UNGODLY EMPIRE

By

AERON KURY

Sonoman Publishing

0

A Note from the Author

"This book gives a very realistic and horrifying look into one very possible future, if the human race doesn't change the destructive direction their currently heading towards. But it also has an insightful message of hope for humanity."

A Window into the Future!

His name is Jonathan Towers. He's the leader of the underground movement, that's resisting the Noble World Alliance, or what they refer to as the "Ungodly Empire", from destroying the Planet, eliminating God, and suppressing the human race of love, liberty and spiritual freedom.

In your near future, the struggle with mankind's petroleum technology reaches a critical point of self-destruction, when the World leaders continue to allow corporations to keep abusing the Planet with fossil fuel pollution and deforestation, ignoring the dire warnings from the scientific community. Although many people already had an overwhelming feeling that they were heading for the complete annihilation of the planet, the World leaders and the large corporations still aggressively pursued this destructive path in the name of financial profit.

Many people were caught up into advancing their careers and making money so they can purchase the good life. Almost everyone wanted to have the current advancements in technology, the latest fashions, biggest houses, and the best automobiles. They were not really concerned, but aware of the disasters and diseases that were threatening human life, and what was causing it.

Society was distracted with materialism, and admiration of their own creations.

Then the massive damage to the environment unexpectedly came in a continuous wave of natural disasters, like plagues from God, which swept across the planet. There was an extreme draught followed by unprecedented wildfires, devastating earthquakes, and volcanic eruptions.

The sea levels rose and warmed, leading to the near extinction of fish as a food supply. In addition, a large portion of the drinkable water also became contaminated.

All of these environmental disasters had a dramatic effect on the world's food production. *Eventually there wasn't enough food to feed 7 Billion people.* The remaining water and farmlands could only produce enough food to feed two-thirds of that amount.

Economies collapsed, riots and pandemonium ensued, and millions of people were killed when a barbarous form of martial law had to be implemented. The World was about to plunge into War over food and water.

World leaders knew if they went to war, it would be nuclear, and that would create a terrifying holocaust. The radiation fallout would absolutely make this already grim situation much worse. They desperately wanted to prevent this from happening, because no one would benefit from a nuclear war.

The majority of Christians, Jews and Muslims believed it was a punishment from God for Man's greedy, sinful, and destructive ways of life. But the scientist had concluded that these disasters were the effects from global warming.

World leaders had an emergency meeting and the three major world powers, Demetri Butinov of Russia, Xi Chang of China, and Ronald Spade of the USA, decided to join together and take control over all existing private farm lands, food production facilities, and water supplies. They also seized control of gas and oil supplies. This coalition became the "Noble World Alliance" (NWA).

Russia and China shared power equally while the leader of the USA followed their lead. The NWA asserted that God and religion were to blame for the disasters that caused the catastrophic food shortage, and economic collapse. They decided to *"Outlaw Religion!"* This sent a shock wave of disbelief and outrage throughout the religious communities. And they forcibly silenced all the scientists from making any more claims that global warming caused the disasters.

The NWA spearheaded the restructuring of the World's economy, and the enforcement of this new international law.

The Judicial system would continue to uphold the common laws for offenses like theft, assault etc...The prisons were turned into slave labor camps, like the Russian Gulags, for the low level criminals who accepted the chip to work on infrastructure projects, but all the dangerous criminals were immediately executed.

The Constitution was void. Democracies no longer functioned. They confiscated all private citizens' personal weapons. People no longer had the right to bear arms, only military personnel are allowed to have weapons. Most of the other countries followed along with this movement, because no other country could stand up against the Three Super Powers once they joined their military forces together. The NWA took control of the Internet to censor the flow of information and e-commerce activity. They also took control of all media broadcast facilities and movie studios. There was no longer any idolized Hollywood stars and their movies.

The NWA destroyed all movies and music that were produced in the free world era.

Then a new worldwide credit based commerce system was set up and implemented. People would earn credits as they worked a job within the petroleum industrial community to purchase goods and services. It's basically the same jobs people were working before the collapse like manufacturing, distribution, construction, military, government, education and communications...But now with a different method of operation and purpose.

The stock market no longer existed after the government takeovers of private businesses, and banks became Credit Management Facilities. There was no longer any need for cash.

The only way people could work, buy, sell or trade was to pledge allegiance to the NWA and have a Bio-Chip embedded in their forehands. When the Bio-Chip is scanned, that person's file would appear on the screen.

It contained all of his or her personal information, classification, and credit earnings.

Anyone who did not renounce their God and take the Bio-Chip would not be able to purchase food, water, transportation, utilities, services, and obtain or retain housing.

Every country that joined the NWA used their nation's armies and police forces to implement this new system on their own citizens. They enforced the new law of the land, utilizing the "state of the art" surveillance systems to track and eradicate the threat of the new enemy without any oversight restrictions. These changes in the social structure came very quickly, and it was an emotionally exhausting and extremely difficult task to complete.

This created a deadly struggle for people of faith to maintain their religious practices, and The Noble World Alliance to eradicate, what they perceived, as a threat to their industrial lifestyle.

Friends and families were being torn apart and *the emotional pain of these dramatic changes was devastating to the continuation of civilized human societies.*

The NWA destroyed most of the religious buildings and burned their pious books. The church owned properties were turned into "Conversion Processing Centers." They were similar to concentration camps, and military squads were sent out regularly to round people up to either convert or exterminate them. When you were captured, they would allow a grace period for the detainees to choose conversion, if you did not, then you were executed. They use a variety of brutal execution methods like firing squads, beheadings, and medieval crucifixions.

There are different groups of people rejecting the Bio-Chip. Most of the Buddhist, Hindus, Muslims, and Jews converted, but small groups of them were resisting. They make up the European and Persian resistance.

The largest religious group resisting is the Christians, and they call themselves the "Natural Earth Liberators" (NEL).

Jonathan was able, with guidance from the Holy Spirit, to unify the people who had the courage and strength to resist the NWA and reject the bio chip. They believe that they're stewards of God's Earth, and must *protect the environment* from the people who perpetuate the destructive petroleum industrial system. They blame them for damaging the Planet, and poisoning the people with cancer and diseases.

Jonathan got them organized and started carrying out missions to shut down destructive environmental activities, and infiltrate food storage warehouses in order to obtain food and supplies to survive.

They also find ways to broadcast their message of spiritual awareness and freedom on the autocratically controlled communication networks.

They believe that the prophecies from the Bible are coming true, with the end time tribulations happening, and the beast rising to force people to take the mark. So they are targeted by the NWA as the main threat and would viciously cut off their heads to send an intimidating message, and because they possibly believe that they might resurrect from the dead.

The NEL followers now have to live in secret societies. There's a spirit of unity within the NEL community. Even though they're considered to be a pack of outcasts, they share mutual respect and love for one another.
The members feel a deeply emotional and spiritual connection within the group. They have a "What affects you-affects me," attitude.

They're all part of the same spiritual body, sharing everything according to the individual needs of each member. It took these extreme conditions to bring them clarity of right and wrong, and reach this level of morality.

They will protect the Earth from the NWA who doesn't seem to care if they destroy it, and prevent them from oppressing their spiritually free souls, and eliminating their belief in "God" the all powerful creator.

They now live with a passionate purpose and no longer feel the depression, ugliness, and emptiness they felt while living within the confines of the Industrial community.

They had to shed the destructive mentality that was leading mankind to its demise with their factories, engines, machines and pollution. They believe they're in the next phase of mankind's tribulations that will eventually lead to the Eternal Kingdom, free from the corrupt authoritarian regime. They no longer fear death, but embrace an afterlife.

But they're still brutally hunted on a daily basis, like when Roman Emperor Nero was mercilessly exterminating Christian's!

The Noble World Alliance just wants to keep the petroleum industrial system operating at all costs. They don't want to change a lifestyle which they're accustomed to, even if it's Destroying them!

There's a brutal and ruthless General, who looks similar to Himmler, named Pacstabus who's in charge of all oppressive missions and operations in North America. His main priority is to protect the NWA's interest, and eliminate any resistance.

He enjoys watching people suffer. One of his morbid hobbies is reading about Josef Mengele's abominable experimental surgeries on humans in the death camps. Torturous methods of persuasion are common practice. They are extremely sadistic, violent and immoral. Just like the Nazis behaved during their atrocious reign.

Everybody's deepest loyalties would be put to the test.

People didn't seem to realize that it was more important to protect and sustain the natural resources, and life on Earth, than to defend the petroleum industry that was destroying it. Most of the people were more interested in, "The World and all its Glory", and not "The Earth and all its Beauty."

The space scientists spent too much time and money on their back-up plan; trying to make space station colonies, and terraforming Mars to make it sustainable for human life.

They should have been concentrating on solving the problems on Earth! Time ran out for the space scientist.

Space stations and Mars was *not* the solution! Food and drinkable water are now in short supply, and people are desperately fighting just to obtain these vital resources. This brings us to Jonathan's nightmarish reality,

Which is present day mankind's near future!

C1

It's a hot muggy day in December, and it seems more like summer than winter. Today the clouds have a very distraught shape, almost as if they're expressing grief and sadness, as the wind blows them across the faded sky. A Cessna jet plane roars through the distressed airspace, as the occupants sadly gaze out the window at a section of the California landscape that is now scorched and destroyed because of the devastating Earthquakes and Wild Fires.

Most of the northern area of the state looks more like a war-torn battlefield, rather than the beautiful paradise that it once was. All the highly coveted, and prestigious beach front coastal communities no longer exist, due to the sea level rising. The central and southern parts of the state are still habitable.

The plane starts to carefully descend, and safely lands at the Los Angeles International Airport. A caravan of government vehicles leaves the airport with its important cargo, and is now speeding down the main interstate to avoid any possible assassination attempts from hostilely disgruntled citizens.

The heavily guarded caravan arrives at its destination and quickly drives through the gate, and pulls up to the front of the new State Capitol Building, which was previously the Getty Museum. It's late in the afternoon, around three thirty.

The museum has been transformed into a luxurious meeting facility, where the heads of state gather to discuss and address critical issues within their region.

A tall distinguished looking man with dark physical features, and a very serious expression on his weathered face, steps out of the limousine that was being protected by the caravan.

He delightfully smells the odor of charred remains that still lingers in the air from the previous wild fire disaster, like a pleasing aroma, as he briskly walks towards the facility.

His name is Davidson McCormick; he's well educated, very powerful, and comes from a prominent, wealthy family.
He is a direct descendant of the Rockefellers. He is the ambassador of the western territory, in the country that was formerly known as the United States. Now it's just referred to as North American. There are no longer 49 separate states and Canada, now there are ten North American regions.

Each individual region is ruled by an ambassador, who presides over the governors of each state within his territory. The individual states still kept their original names, California, Texas, New York etc...The ambassadors rule with an iron rod, and utilize the military division assigned to each of their territories to make sure they're carrying out the oppressive will of the Noble World Alliance (NWA).

It's utterly a brutal Military Police Country! The ten ambassadors report directly to the Monarch of North America. There are seven monarchs, one for each of these alliance countries; North America, South America, England, Italy, Iran, India, and Africa. England's Monarch reigns over the United Kingdom, France and Spain, while the Italian Monarch rules over Italy, Greece and the Mediterranean.

The Seven Monarchs are controlled by the Russian Dictator, Demetri Butinov, who also took over the Scandinavian countries and made them part of Russia. He's an average size Caucasian man with white thinning hair, but has a soft innocence that almost hides his ruthless disposition.

He works in close collaboration with The Chinese Emperor Xi Chang, who presides over all the Asian territories; China, Indochina, Japan, and the Koreas.

The State of Israel exists no longer. The Iranians and Pakistanis invaded, backed by Russia. The Israelis ironically launched a nuclear missile, in their pathetic defense, that was quickly intercepted by the Russians.
Their cherished Wailing Wall was demolished by the Iranian Monarch after they shamelessly conquered Israel. The humiliated Jews, that didn't convert, were disgracefully re-scattered to the wailing winds of deep distress.

The Monarch of Iran controls all the Persian Territories. He has been also attempting to eliminate the Muslim resistance, which is lead by Mustafa Rahman. Mexico and Central America have been left out of the alliance, and they have become a lawless battlefield for the gangs and cartels. They refer to this territory as Mexoamerica.

When the food shortage had its catastrophic impact on the world it brought out a different side of people's character.

The basic instinct of survival took over, and people turned into selfish savages when faced with the possibility of starvation and death.

The once prideful and arrogant Americans were reduced to disenchanted, animalistic, self-centered survivalists. There were good hearted compassionate people that tried to hold on to their humanity as long as they could, but that was quickly stripped away as the NWA took its ruthless galvanizing grip on this cold new world. The only way to retain your humanity was to reject the Bio-Chip, and join the underground.

Ambassador Davidson is an atheist and believes religion is a form of brain washing that divides societies rather than bringing them together, by preaching arrogance and exclusivity that theirs is "the true religion and the others are heretics."

He blames organized religion for most of the damaging social conflicts that had complicated civilized man's existence on Earth, and *does not believe petroleum pollution is harming the planets environment.*

He believes religion is "the opiate of the masses." And a belief in God, without objectively verifiable proof, is like believing in superheros like Batman or the Avenger. He absolutely hates religion! He believes the underground members are all contemptuous traitors.

Near the State Building, there's a group of converted people who regularly meet in secrecy to have a Bible study at an abandoned house, with no electricity or electronic devices. Candles light the room, and cast a menagerie of eerie shadows on the walls.

They're all very scared and paranoid, as they listen to helicopter patrols meticulously monitor activities from above. They think their group may have been compromised, and if they're caught, it would mean immediate and painful death for all participants. This is just like it was when the disciples were hiding after Jesus was crucified. One of the members says, "Blessed are the passive believers, for they shall inherit the Earth."

There's a strange sounding noise outside, like cracking branches, the group stops reading and stays silent for a moment.... then continues, "Blessed is the sad in spirit from enduring evil, for theirs is the Kingdom of Heaven."

They hear another strange sound and cautiously pause. One of the members quickly gets up to look out the window, doesn't see anything and rejoins the group.

They continue, "Blessed are you when people insult you, persecute you and falsely say all kinds of evil things against you because of the Lord." The reader pauses and with a delighted tone continues, "Rejoice and be glad, because great is your reward in heaven, for, in the same way, they persecuted the prophets who came before you." Then suddenly they hear a loud voice coming out of megaphone and the enforcer militantly says, "You are surrounded, *do not* attempt to come out or you will be shot." The study group goes silent, and there's a moment of uncertainty.

Then an incendiary grenade comes crashing through the window, and lands on the floor.

Startled, they all look at it, and then look up at each other for a brief moment of disbelief.

Then one of the members says, "Don't forgive them father for they *know* what they do!" and then the grenade mercilessly explodes, viciously burning all the members to death.

The Ambassador is here to conduct some very sensitive NWA business. California is prominently a shipping port for the predominant commerce activity in the Western Pacific Region, but also has movie studios and broadcasting facilities for propaganda purposes.

Ambassador Davidson majestically walks up the ascending stairs, and enters the historical building. He briskly asks the petite receptionist, "Is everybody in the conference room?"

She quickly replies, "Yes Sir!"

He continues walking towards the meeting room. Once inside, he slowly makes his way to the podium at the front of the room, and gazingly looks out at all the governors as they attentively await his inspiring words.

Then with a casual, but serious tone Davidson says, "Our first order of business is addressing the theft problem at the food distribution locations. I want to increase the number of officers at each location. Anyone caught stealing food shall be shot on sight."

The governors acknowledge the Ambassadors demand. Then he continues, "Next, we must secure the southern border...We need to reinforce the wall and increase patrols at the border to keep those savagely violent gangs from infiltrating our country. We must prevent them from spreading their chaos and murderous terror."

They said the drug wars were bad, but now it's ten times worse. The Ambassador continues, "Soon the Monarch plans to exterminate all the people in the southern lawless territory of Mexoamerica, so we need to protect the border a little while longer. They will not be given the option to accept the Bio-Chip."

The Monarch of North America, Ronald
Spade, a large masterful man with light hair,
and his top military adviser, General Pacstabus,
who's as ruthless as Julius Caesar was during his
campaigns to expand the Roman Empire, are
sitting in the Oval office discussing an
eradication strategy.

The General with a very serious tone says,
"Sir, I believe the most effective plan is to send
in a squadron of bombers, and drop Sarin gas.
That will eliminate the people, but keep the
structures intact. The crows and vultures will
clean up the mess for us."

Monarch Spade responds, "I agree General;
I'm fed up with their atrocities, they're nothing
but an irritating thorn in my ass.
I'll talk to Butinov, and I don't think he'll have a
problem with this. We're going to make the
world glorious again!" He looks at the General
and jokingly says, "I feel sorry for those crows. "
The underlying truth is it also gives them an
opportunity to reduce the population, because
overpopulation is a very serious problem.

C2

Back at The Capitol Building, the Ambassador continues, "Our next order of business is; we must eliminate this futile attempt of resistance...The underground continues to shut down productive industrial developments, hijack food shipments, and spreading negative propaganda about the NWA...They continue to perpetuate this absurd myth about an all powerful Omni-present God that will supposedly come down from the heavens, and save them from the Earth damaging evil oppressors!" He takes a breath, and then says with a disbelieving tone, "The NEL blames *us* for all the environmental and health problems, and blatantly disrespect the industrial revolutionist's, like my great great grandfather, that helped build this tremendous society!"

Then with a stern look on his face says, "The undergrounds very existence is an insult to the unified coalition, and our luxurious way of life... I can feel their defiant spirit in the opinionated air, like a constantly ringing bell that irritably bashes on my brain."

The Governor of Colorado responds, "Sir, we have been assisting the ABI with our complete cooperation." The FBI is now referred to as the ABI (Alliance Bureau of Investigations). Then California governor Clovis adds, "We will silence the voice of Anarchy and cut down the Tree of God!"

Clovis comes from a long lineage of politicians, his father and grandfathers were highly respected Senators before the collapse. Ambassador Davidson slams the podium and shouts, "We must continue to eliminate the defiant pious parasites with Extreme Prejudice! Dictator Butinov says he believes that their God brought all these destructive plagues and misery to our world, and wants us to destroy them...Either way, there is no place in the new world order for those insubordinate, non-submissive religious zealots who believe in a nonexistent, make believe God!" Then a unified roar resonates from the room as they all experience an overwhelming emotional wave of joyous hatred.

This reminds the Ambassador about the recent fall of modern Rome, when the Russians expressed a similar hatred towards the Catholic Church as they invaded the Vatican. The Vatican's armed forces, the Swiss Guard, were absolutely no match for "The Russian Military Beast."

The merciless invasion lasted one day until they shamelessly surrendered.

The entire event was televised. They publically disrobed and humiliated the priests. They destroyed most of their priceless religious art, and burned the pious books in the Vatican's extensive library. The Pope was brutally executed on a live TV broadcast!

Most of the Cardinals and Bishops converted after that happened. The hierarchy that didn't convert was either savagely tortured and killed, or got away and joined the European resistance. The Russian Federation immediately made the Vatican their new home.
They transformed it into their main operations center for the top ranking Kremlin officials, or the "Kremlin de la crème."

The Ambassador continues, "We are going to add more sensitive sensors along the off route state crossing areas, increase drone patrols, and upgrade facial technology at the check points." He passes out flash drives with the details and programs for the security improvements.

The governors quickly take the flash drives and then he continues, "We need to find out who's leading this movement, so be sure to thoroughly interrogate all captured underground members, and get me the name of their leader!

They can be identified by a tattoo of an Eagle on their wrist where the Bio-Chip would have been injected. We need to cut off the head of the Eagle!" Then the Ambassador briefly pauses and takes a drink from a glass of water and endearingly says,

"Long live the Serpent! Praise to the Dragon."

The governors repeat his praise.

Then the Ambassador cheerfully says, "Now that our business is finished, I have brought my personal chef and he's preparing us a spectacular Mediterranean meal so "Let the festivities begin!"

They all partake in a celebratory feast, eating a variety of gourmet foods, and drinking the finest wines brought in from the Ambassador's personal stock, as they listen to a live band performing erotically seductive music. The ancient old spirit of fleshly pleasures arises inside of them. Male and female prostitutes, young and old, are brought into the conference room for governors to feed their perverted sexual appetite.

They continue until the early morning hours indulging and pleasuring themselves in a variety of sexually immoral activities, just like one of Roman Emperor Caligula's Wild Orgy Parties.

The next day, the Ambassador and his governors are getting ready to attend the most popular sport in North America called, "Battleball." It's basically football, but it's played more violently, like the Gladiator games of ancient Rome.

Players are allowed to injure each other during the execution of a play, as they attempt to get the ball into the opposing team's end zone.

The players risk getting critical injuries like broken limbs, paralyzed, or even brain damage. They allow individual players to fight if they have a penalty issue. The crowds love it when they do. Sometimes it escalates to the point when all players are involved, like a gang fight. There's a squad of enforcers on the sidelines to monitor these fights if they get out of control.

As they're heading towards the stadium, the Ambassador thinks about his strict father's method of discipline, and tough love he imposed on him, to instill a sense of accountability and diligence into his character. He remembers one time in particular when his father had a very violent outburst because Davidson took his father's favorite car, a rare 1963 Ferrari GTO worth 70 million dollars, to a high school football game without permission, and when he found out, he beat him severely with a deep sea fishing rod. His father would say, "I'm doing this is for your own good...and it brings me no pleasure." This was one of the odd comments his father made that he found to be very puzzling; because his father seemed to be enjoying it. He still has the hideous scars on his back.

On the way to the stadium they pass a food distribution facility that has an uninvitingly long line of extremely unhappy patrons waiting to purchase basic food supplies: bread, eggs, milk,

rice, beans fruits, vegetables, and bottled water, because tap water is undrinkable. Meat and seafood are considered a luxury, and are very hard to acquire. Your monthly credit allotment determines how well you eat. Inside the store, there are armed guards strategically positioned around the facility to discourage theft. A retired war veteran named Glenn Miller is at the register trying to purchase food.
The attendant scans the chip and his account reads zero credits. The attendant informs him, and he angrily responds,
"I risked my life to protect this damn country, and now I can't purchase any food because you say I have no more fucking credits, are you kidding me!?"
Now he's extremely upset and says, "I should blow this store and your damn credit system straight to HELL!"
The attendant feverishly presses a button; an alarm rings as guards swarm to her register.

She frightfully tells the guards, "This man
threatened to blow up the store."
They forcibly grab the disgruntled veteran, and
quickly haul him away.

C3

    Desperate hungry beggars are crowded around the exits, trying to get a sympathetic handout. One panhandler holds a sign that says, "Will trade a kidney for food." There are no longer any independent or corporate grocery stores with a variety of different brand name products. Now it's just Alliance stores with their brand-products. There are separate stores for the other perishable products.

    An anxious looking man, named Brian Cheeves, with a cart full of groceries hurriedly leaves the store to avoid annoying beggars or violent muggers, like he's transporting precious cargo. He's hoping to return home safely to his family without any hostile confrontations. A lot of people now have deep rooted anger issues, and he has learned the hard way, that they are easily provoked into violent reactions.

He makes it to his minivan, quickly puts the bags in the back, and then speeds away.

There are people who have taken the Bio Chip, but are unable to work, so they have to live in an area referred to as "Camp Dread." It's an absolutely horrible place to live.
It's a tent city with plastic outhouses scattered everywhere, with no electricity or running water. There are half dead people, some with infected soars all over their bodies, just wondering around in a confused haze, like night of the living dead.

All the people living there are malnourished and are forced to eat dogs, rats, and other repulsive vermin. There are also rumors of cannibalism taking place in these gruesome areas.

You'll know when you're coming near these camps, because the stench of decrepit flesh mixed with human excrement blows in the tainted breeze, and when you smell it, you get this absolutely disgusting and nauseated feeling.

Brian Cheeves, a clean cut management type, works as a stage manager for The National Broadcasting Center. He is married with three children, two boys, Mason thirteen, Liam five, and a girl named Isabella who is nine years old. He pulls into the driveway of his modest three bedroom house. He enters, and his family is in the living room watching Alliance censored shows on TV. He loves his family very much. His beautiful Spanish wife, Olivia, looks at him with an extremely unhappy expression. She has been struggling with depression and has attempted suicide. She hasn't been sleeping well because of her demonized nightmares. With an exhausted look, she says, "What have we become? Where does this sick ugly feeling come from? What did I do wrong?"

Brian compassionately stares and then replies, "You didn't do anything wrong... Why do you feel that way?"

She stares back at him for an uncomfortable moment, with a confused look on her face.

He walks into the kitchen and puts away the food. "I feel like I've betrayed someone" she softly says. Brian, slightly irritated responds, "Do we have to get into this right now? Okay, who did you betray?" he caringly asked. There's another uncomfortable moment of silence and she starts scratching the scar where the Bio Chip was implanted.
"I Don't Know! Maybe God?" she starts crying and it deeply saddens him.

"Olivia honey, did you take your medication?" He concerningly asked. There's a silence, she holds up the pill bottle, and then with a soothingly calm tone Brian says, "Good... would you like me to cook you up some spaghetti tonight?" She nods her head as though she's surrendering, and then looks away.

You can hear the TV in the background, and the announcer is introducing the teams for the next Battleball game that is about to begin. Tonight the Vicious Jaguars are battling the Wicked Ravens.

Every region has eight teams, and they play by process of elimination to find out who will be the Eastern and Western Champions. Then a final game is played, but now they call it "The Ultimate Battle."

The Ambassador and his governors arrive at the stadium and make their way up to the private clubhouse. They enter and immediately see the graffiti on the walls that says, "Live Strong and Die Free, NEL Eternally"
The ambassador feels truly violated and humiliated. He furiously says, "How did those goddamn Eco-terrorist get in here?" The Battleball game punctually begins.

Back at the Cheeves house, the family has just finished eating their spaghetti dinner. Brian excuses the children from the table and tells them to go up to their room to study.
Then he looks at his wife and concerningly says, "I think you need to go back and see the Dr." she dreadfully replies, "I hate going to the hospital, the doctors don't care.

They're just looking for the quick fix...or they want to put you out to pasture."

If the Doctor labels someone as "expired" that means they are fatally ill and the Hospital won't treat them anymore. For example, if you have terminal cancer, they don't try to keep you alive with chemotherapy.
If you don't have a family to take care of you, then they will send you "out to pasture" or what the medical community refers to as "Euthanasia." They have done away with unnecessary life support system applications. The Doctors will no longer sustain someone's life if they are terminally ill or fatally injured from an accident.

They will only treat someone if they're mentally or physically fixable to continue working. When someone's dying from complications of old age, they don't keep trying to revive them; they will just let them die. The medical staff is emotionally disconnected, and they treat patients like soulless slabs of meat.

Sadly, there is no compassion or empathy anymore in medical communities.

The doctors are like butchers, because they handle patients like sides of beef, and they manage the hospital like a car being repaired in an auto body shop. Some people derogatorily refer to them as, "Body Shop Butchers." There are no longer any private practices or independent medical facilities. It's now a nationalized healthcare system.

The Hippocratic Oath no longer applies.

If someone speaks out and blames the Alliance for their psychological or emotional distress, then they're flagged as a possible sympathizer, and put on heavy medications like Thorazine or clozapine to subdue them. If that doesn't work, then you're sent to a readjustment program. They claim that it's a humane program, but it's basically a torturous brain washing technique. The patient is sent to a maximum security mental health facility, where they and are locked down in their rooms.

Subliminal spoken word recordings, instilling positive reinforcement messages, are hauntingly playing their repetitive chant over the intercom system day and night. They can hear words like obey, submit, and conform to the will of the Alliance and you will be content. They have a daily schedule of aggressive mental restructuring sessions to reprogram their logic, and make them believe the resistance is causing their guilt and depression.

The process usually takes twenty-one grueling days to complete the "neurowash." If that doesn't work, then they electronically lobotomize the patient, which can be extremely devastating and burdensome to the immediate family. Brian compassionately says to his wife, "I wish I knew how to free you from this demoralizing spirit that has a powerful grip on your soul," and with a conflicting feeling of love and frustration, he passionately hugs her.

Back at the clubhouse, the Ambassador and his governors are staring at the graffiti. The Ambassador is too upset to enjoy the game. Governor Clovis fearfully says, "My deepest apologies ambassador, I'll make sure to check the video footage personally and identify the criminals...I'll download their faces in the recognition system so we can quickly apprehend those insolent Eco-terrorist and execute them."

The Ambassador stares at him with an ancient fire in his eyes, and anger that was drudged up from the bottomless pit and says, "Someone will pay for this barbaric act of disrespect!"

At the mental hospital Dr. Baumann is preparing for his first patient of the day. A techy looking man, named Drake Jackson, who works as an engineer at the drone manufacturing facility walks into his office. He's extremely psychotic, with deep rooted fear issues. The Doctor says, "Please sit down." He sits down on the leather recliner and grabs the handle, then cranks back the chair.

Drake believes that the Aliens are responsible for everything that's going on in the world. In his previous session, he told the Doctor that they follow him around in their cloaked spaceships, consistently monitoring him, to make sure he doesn't notice them. They don't want to be revealed. They want to remain invisible. Anyone who can see them will be abducted. If they can do a successful memory wipe, then they'll return you to earth, if not, then you become their property.

The aliens don't like to abduct too many humans because that might bring attention to their existence.

He also claims, the aliens can possess humans, and make them do things on their behalf without anyone knowing it was them.

The Doctor asks "How are you holding up?"

"By a very thin layer of gravity," Drake disturbingly laughs and says, "Well... I haven't been abducted yet; do you know why?"

The Doctor nods and curiously asks "Why?"

He seriously responds, "It's because I never look directly at them."

"Oh...them? What do "them" look like Drake? Are they the Greys, The Reptilians or the Arcturians?" He curiously asked. Drake frustratingly replies, "No! The Pleiadians and the Greens! They're fighting against one another for Galactic dominance.

Planet Earth is the most important planet, because it generates eternal souls. The more souls they gather, the more powerful they become."

The Doctor plays along and acceptingly says, "Okay, I see...Why they want to remain invisible?"

Drake arrogantly answers, "Because if they're sighted by humans, then the Supreme leader of all the Universes will ground them...And being grounded is extremely torturous to these beings, because the exploration of infinite space is what they enjoy doing."

The doctor thinks to himself, this is almost believable and says, "Very interesting."

Back at the Battleball game; it's now in the last quarter, and you can hear the announcers excitingly talking about a player who was critically injured, "That looked like a real back breaker!" The announcer sarcastically said. The medical cart hauls the disabled player off the field as the crowd loudly cheers.

The game continues with more injuries and fights, as the spectators are morbidly amused with the violent game. The game ends, and the Ravens have decimated the Jaguars.

Then Governor Clovis says, "Don't worry Sir, I want to reassure you that I will make it my top priority to find the criminals who violated our clubhouse."

Ambassador Davidson furiously replies, "I want their heads on an Iron spiked platter, and if not, then I want yours!"

He stares at the governor with an extremely displeasing look, and then pulls out a Cohiba Cuban cigar and lights it.

C4

Jonathan Towers, the esteemed, well educated leader of the underground, wakes up in hot sweat after having a vivid dream about a horrifying creature. It was about a Dragon that had seven heads, with ten horns on each head, and a crown on each horn. Each individual head could blow fire that brutally burns its victims, but doesn't kill them, unless they're eaten. He lies in bed, still half asleep, reflecting on the dream, wondering what it means.

He stares up at the ceiling and sees a spider making his way to the other side. It makes him think back when he was younger and how he used to collect spiders as a hobby. He was fascinated about the way they would weave their webs, and then they just sit and wait for an unknowing victim to get tangled in it.

It makes him forget about his dream for a couple of minutes. He gets up and goes to the bathroom to take a leak, washes off his face and pulls his mind out of the dream state. It's an important day for the Natural Earth Liberators (NEL) and he needs to get focused.

They're going to meet with a resistance sympathizer, or what they call "Gracers." Gracers are people that have already taken the chip but regret it, like there in a state of grace. This Gracer is going to give them classified Information they need to complete their next mission.

He gets dressed and goes into the kitchen where some of the other crew members are getting themselves something to eat. Jimmy Fitz, the tall ex-marine, and a good ole country boy from the mid-west, is cooking some scrambled eggs in an old iron skillet and jokingly says, "This is my special recipe that pacified a platoon."

While he was serving in the marines, he was deployed to Iraq, and one day the cooks in the mess tent got really sick with the flu. So no one had cooked breakfast for the hungry soldiers, and all the men were getting very agitated and upset.

Jimmy stepped up and cooked breakfast for everyone and calmed them down with his special recipe. They say it had a very unique secret ingredient. That's how he got his nickname, "the pacifier."

He served a couple of tours during the Iraq War. He suffered from post traumatic stress syndrome because of the atrocities he observed. One of the worse incidents that he experienced that almost pushed him over the edge, into insanity, was when they bombed a facility they thought was full of hostels, but it was civilians.

The scene was utter carnage; he put down his weapon and started to help dig survivors and bodies out of the rubble.

The worst part is when He found a blood drenched torso from a little boy; he started vomiting profusely and then broke down and began sorrowfully weeping.

   After that, Jimmy wasn't the same anymore. He refused orders to continue fighting. He was put in the stockade and then was dishonorably discharged.

Jimmy says to Jonathan, "Are you ready for something eggsquisite."

Jonathan gives him a smile even though it's a corny joke, because he likes to see his crew in good spirits. He sits down at the kitchen table and starts to eat his eggs.

   He grabs for the salt, but it slips out his hands. He has a flashback and remembers a time when he was at a restaurant with his old girlfriend Janea, and she said with a very sexy tone, "If you pass me the salt, I'll be the spice in your life." The remark caught him off guard; it was just a silly, funny moment, but he can't seem to forget it.

He starts to eat his eggs and refocus's on the task at hand.

They're going to meet with up with one of Jonathan's old history students, who now works for the national broadcasting facility. He is the Gracer, and his name is Steven Ferris. He's a very skilled and talented computer engineer. He's a skinny, nerdy looking man who's part Asian and part French. He's going to give them access codes and blueprints to enter the facility, and assist them with their next mission.

Jonathan is planning to make a pirate broadcast, because people can no longer post personal videos on the internet. All media activities are thoroughly monitored by the NWA. Freedom of Speech is *prohibited!* Broadcast centers are the only facilities that have the capability to upload videos, and transmit shows that people can view.

If you want to access the internet, you need to have your chip scanned, and then you're allowed to view *approved material* or to conduct ecommerce.

Jonathan wants to "Open the eyes of the blinded masses." And he also says, "We need to lift the clouds of deception from there site, and free them from the dragons destructive spell."

The irony of their situation is that the NWA, who won't let go of their harmful mindset, keep espousing there polluting petroleum way of life and still believe that, "It's improving their quality of life" and "making it more convenient," when actually it's poisoning, and killing them in the process of sustaining it.

They are under an extremely powerful spell that blinds, and keeps them in a deep, dark, state of denial. Most of the people who have accepted the Bio chip are depressingly unhappy and living in a state of constant fear. He wants to liberate them from their agonizing existence.

At this point, the NWA has converted around fifty-five percent of the population. First they converted people they needed to maintain the new economical industrial structure. But now they're on an aggressive campaign to convert or eliminate the rest of the population.

He finishes his eggs, and sits back for a minute. He asks Jimmy, "How's our food supply?"

"Enough for about another month" Jimmy replied.

Jonathan believes that an important part of the message from the Messiah was; "everything should be shared equally and accordingly to the individual needs of each member."

He thinks about the time before the collapse happened when he was a well-respected college teacher, and taught History at the University of California. Jonathan was fascinated with ancient civilizations; from the Samarians, to the Egyptians, Mayans, Persians, Greeks, and the Imperial Romans.

He was also intrigued by the early Europeans like Charlemagne and the Holy Roman Empire, Mohamed and Islam, Napoleon with the French Empire, Genghis Khan, and the Mongolian Empire, and of course Hitler's Germany. He noticed they all shared something in common; it seems they all have been strongly influenced by some supernatural force that compelled them to want to set out to conquer, and rule the world. What Jonathan refers to as the dragon's delusive spell.

The main reason he was so intrigued with history was because of the idea that if he can understand what happened in the past, he would be able to see what's coming in the future. He also recognized a strange similarity among the ancient civilizations, and how they all wrote about these mysterious sky beings, which were consistently interacting with the people on Earth. The various civilizations had different names for them like, the Annunaki, Amun-Ra, Vishnu, and Kukulkan.

The book of Enoch refers to them as "The Fallen Angels." There was Azaayel who taught men how to make weapons, Tamiel who taught astronomy, Amazarak who taught sorcery, and Uzza and Azza who taught them mathematics and science.

These beings from the sky that traveled around in their chariots of fire, seemed to have stopped interacting with mankind for the time being, but you can still see the effects of their contributions. Jonathan thinks they're all talking about the same beings. He believes they are the fallen angels. They have introduced knowledge and technology, against the will of God that have influenced the direction of civilizations throughout history, which eventually seems to lead to a catastrophic end.

But he also knows about the righteous angels like Michael, Gabriel, and Raphael who assist God in the battle against Satan and the fallen. Angels have the ability to transform into flesh and blood humans to interact with people, but the fallen can no longer have this ability.

They can only invisibly influence and possess other humans. He stops reflecting and thinks about the collapse, and the rise of the current horrifying Ungodly Empire.

He has a moment of anxiety and disbelief, but that quickly passes. He slowly gets up from the kitchen table and goes to the sink and washes his dishes, and then goes into the living room.

C5

In the living room of the four bedroom safe house, hidden somewhere in the dense forest of Northern Colorado is Keshaun Darren, the well built black ex football star, who is sitting on a faded second hand couch. He was a Muslim who converted to Christianity.

Jonathan playfully says, "What's shaking KD"?

Keshaun answers, "The unstable foundations of society." Then he says, "So, when are you gonna layout the plans for this next mission, my man."

Jonathan responds, "I'll tell you what's going on when everyone gets in here"

Keshaun use to play professional football for the Denver Broncos, before it became Battleball. He was a wide receiver. He loved playing the game. He says, "There's nothing that compares to the intense energy of a sold out stadium full of enthusiastic fans cheering you on".

He was playing in a championship game against the Panthers and he promised his son, who had brain cancer, that he would win the championship for him. In the fourth quarter, during the last minute of the game, with the fans cheering at the top of their lungs, he makes the winning touchdown catch, but his knee was severely injured when he was tackled in the end zone. That ended his career. His son died shortly after that. His life went into a whirlwind spiral downwards.

The only thing that gave him a reason to continue on with life was his anger for the poisons and pollutants that he believed killed his son. This happened prior to the collapse.

Everybody is now in the living room awaiting instructions for their next assignment, after taking a short break from their last successful mission when they synchronized with the other NEL crews, to shut down four major oil refineries at the same time. They blew up the refinery plants control rooms by using remote control drones with C4 strap on them.

Jonathan says to his crew with a serious but hopeful tone, "We're now heading to Los Angeles, where we can access the broadcast centers equipment, and transmit a message of liberation."

About a month ago, Jonathan received an urgent message from the Holy Spirit, in the form of a vision that he needs to deliver to mankind, so he can possibly change the destructive course of events that are soon coming.

Miguel Chavez, the short and stocky ex-con, and ex-gang member, is sitting on the lazy boy chair and sarcastically says,"Aw yes, the mysterious, miraculous, liberating message. L.A., that's my old neighborhood, Mi Barrio...Access or infiltrate?" Jonathan smiles a little. Miguel served 7 years in prison for manslaughter because he was involved in a gang rivalry shot out. A stray bullet from his gun killed an elderly man. While he was incarcerated he got his degree in Religious Studies, and became a born again Christian.

He's one tough Mexican that's not going to renounce his God!

Miguel seriously says, "Do you really think you can change the destructive destination of this misdirected society?...If your interpretations are correct, mankind has just experienced the seven plagues of the trumpets that are written in the Book of Revelations. They match the recent disasters that have just happened. This is God's judgment!"

He makes a sign of the cross on his tattooed chest.

Jonathan sadly replies, "Yes, I do believe this God's judgment...but I'm hoping we can prevent them from continuing, by getting the people to repent and change."

There's a brief moment of silence, and then Miguel asks, "Do you really believe they can change?"

And then Jonathan hopefully responds, "Yes I do! That's why I truly need to deliver this important message."

Then he looks at Jimmy and firmly says, "This is why it's extremely important to figure out the safest route to avoid the checkpoints."

It's more difficult to travel between states lines now, because all the state borders have armed checkpoints, and you need a bio-chip to pass through.

Jimmy acknowledging the seriousness of the situation says, "Jonathan, I know some back roads we could possibly use, I'm pretty sure they're not being patrolled," and then asks, "What time are you going to meet up with Steven?"

Jonathan replies, "Okay, map out a route, and will do a test run to make sure there are no patrols or hidden checkpoints. I'm meeting Steven on the south side of Lake Granby right around sunset."

Ronni Valens eagerly asks, "Can I go with you? We can make it look like we're father and daughter, and I can cover your back."

She's a beautiful bad ass with a sensitive side, and has short spiked black hair.

She used to be an Olympic gymnast and a Buddhist. She had a boyfriend she was deeply in love with, who was an environmental activist.

He went down to the rain forest in South America to help stop deforestation, and got killed in the process by a private security officer, who was working for the corporation funding the cutting. After that, she kind of lost her balance on life's balance beam and gave up gymnastics. To deal with her emotional pain, she did a lot of partying, got some tattoos, became defiant and started rebelling against the industrial system.

Jonathan answers, "Okay, that's a good idea, but dress ordinary."

She usually has a wild fashion style. She wears ripped shirts and shorts, the distressed look, and black combat boots.

Jonathan concernedly says, "Are you sure you can handle it?"

During the last mission, she had a little problem dealing with the stress. Ronni assuredly says, "Don't worry, I won't freak out if we run into a patrol," reassuringly she says, "I can handle it!"

He reluctantly says, "Okay, go and get ready"
Jonathan thinks of her like a daughter.

He starts to think about Janae, the girlfriend he wanted to start a family with. She was a beautiful black woman, with milk chocolate colored skin that was as soft as velvet.
Her bluish green eyes were like the ocean, and they sparkled like the sun reflecting off the water. She had an irresistibly cute, innocent way of talking, which was very erotic to him. He knew there was something very special about her. They meet at a local dance club near the University and immediately felt a magical chemistry between each other. The attraction was mutual. It wasn't a One-sided connection. Sometimes they would just talk for hours about almost anything, but they avoided talking about religion.

As they spent more time with each other, they could feel the emotional bond growing stronger between them, and their feelings became more intensified.

They would share their most intimate thoughts and embarrassing moments at the risk being rejected, and felt an even deeper connection. Because now they're accepting, and trusting each other with the very sensitive information they could use to hurt each other with.

They became best friends and deeply cared for one another, and shared a lot of life experiences together. This grew into one of the most intimately passionate relationships he had ever experienced. He remembers how they loved to go on nature hikes. They would find a special place, surrounded by natural beauty, and then celebrate their discovery with a bottle of aromatic wine, delicious food, and of course a very special dessert. He used to say, "She smells like a strawberry, but taste like an apple." Nature seemed to be their aphrodisiac. One of their most unusual moments happened when they were only six months into their relationship, and they took a trip to the mountains.

That's when she revealed to him her feelings about religion, and she believed "God had brought them together." She said, "I really need to know something that is extremely important to me," he thought she was going to bring up the subject of marriage, but instead said, "Do you truly believe in God?" this caught him by surprise.

She was asking this as if it was a life or death moment. Jonathan didn't know what to say, because he wasn't really sure.

He hesitatingly replied, "I do believe!" but she wasn't really convinced and just said, "A day truly loved by God, is another day truly lived, and I want you to share that with me forever."

But all that came to an end when she contracted leukemia. He had to slowly watch the spirit of life drain out of someone he dearly loved, like a flower withering away.

It broke his heart, the emotional damage he experienced was severe, and his whole world fell apart. He felt like he was being punished, but didn't know why. He got to a point where he didn't care about the daily rituals of life; it all became meaningless to him. That's when he decided to find out what really causes cancer.

His extensive research brought him to the conclusion that carbon pollution was to blame. That's when his disdain began to grow against pollution caused by the industrial system. And then he remembers when he had his first spiritual visitation. An angel that looked like a transparent human figure, appeared to Jonathan in an emotionally intense vivid dream, and told him, "You should be good stewards of the Earth, and protect it from the people who want to destroy it."

He was asleep when the visitation took place, but it felt like he was wide awake, but when he did wake up, it took him a couple of days to understand what had really happened.
Those dramatic events completely changed the direction of his life. That's when he really dedicated his life to understanding God, and

started his crusade against the materialistic, industrial lifestyle. It's different when you say you "believe" something, compared to when you actually believe it. The collapse happened shortly after that.

Ronni comes back and assuredly says, "OK, I'm ready."

Jonathan blithely replies, "Then let's get going, it will take us about six hours round trip, and I want you to drive." Then he inspiringly says to rest of the crew, "When I get back with the Information, we'll work out the details of the plan to make sure the chances of success are in our favor."

Jimmy looks at Jonathan and proudly says, "Live Strong & Die Free, and May the Spirit be with you."

Everyone repeats, "Live Strong & Die Free!"

This is Jonathan's saying which means; to live strong and carry on the way of the wise, and die free from evil oppression. Every time they venture outside, they have to face the reality of being captured, tortured and converted, or killed.

The last thing they want is to conform, and be a part of the Ungodly Empires poisonous industrial machine that destroys, and suppresses the human spirit. They would rather die and go to the land of the dead, and rest their souls until resurrection day.

Most Christians think they go straight to heaven when you die, but this is not what the scriptures state, except for a few worthy people like Elijah and Jesus.

Jonathan thinks about the disciples when they were being hunted for their belief in Jesus, and how it must have felt.

C6

The NWA sends out regular military patrols that are specifically looking for noncons. They are people who haven't been forced to accept the Bio Chip yet. Resisters are what the NWA enforcers are calling people who have rejected the chip and joined the underground.

Jonathan and Ronni get into the electric car and start driving down the road that's lined with beautiful forest trees. He enjoys smelling the scent of pine in the rushing breeze, as they're driving, because it reminds him of freedom. Jonathan sees a dead dog on the side of the road, and remembers when he joined the Sunrise Movement in his early twenties, and they were on their way to Washington D.C. to support new legislation that would end the burning of fossil fuels. He was driving a van, and accidentally hit a dog that was trying to cross the street.

When he got out of the van to check, he saw the dog wasn't moving, but he also noticed it wasn't bleeding. It was a white German shepherd. It looked just like a dog he had when he was seven years old, that he loved very much, who was also hit and killed by a car. That was his first real experience of feeling the pain of losing something he loved.

Then he put his hands on the injured dog's torso, and said a prayer to God, like he was giving the last rites. But then the dog suddenly jumped up, startling him, and quickly ran away. He still wonders whether or not that was a miracle he witnessed.

Ronni noticed Jonathan is deep in thought and curiously asks, "So what are you thinking about?" Jonathan doesn't answer, and continues staring out the window in a mild trance. She quietly keeps driving.

He's now thinking about the time when he was growing up in a lower middle class neighborhood being raised by his mother, because his parents were divorced.

He experienced all the normal insecurities and emotional confusion that most teenagers had to deal with, but he was also caught in the middle of his parent's bitter break up.

He continues thinking about how he had to maintain and manage his inventory of complex emotions without any sound parental guidance. What he wanted most during those years, was to have someone that could help him understand his confusing feelings, and explain the elusive meaning of life to him. He yearned for prudent guidance, a respectable purpose in life, and to belong to something bigger than himself.

But things were a little more difficult for him than other teenagers, because the adults around him had major dysfunctional behavior issues that were being impressed by him. Instead, he had to contend with their twisted lies, hypocrisies, and misguided anger issues without proper intellectual defenses, making his teenage years much more difficult.

He didn't have a good relationship with his father because he would violently and unjustly punish Jonathan for the same mistakes he made, but never took the time to share his experiences and relate to him.

His attitude was, "He's going to prevent Jonathan from making the same mistakes he made, by beating it into him." That was Jonathan's father's warped idea of parental guidance. He was able to survive those frustrating teenage years and develop his emotional heart without any permanent scars.

Jonathan recognized the knowledge he gained through experience. College was his escape from his dysfunctional family situation.

He settled with the understanding that those unpleasant years were preparing him, at an early age, to handle complicated personality issues and adverse situations.

Ronni asks, "Are you alright?"

"Yeah, I'm Okay, just thinking about the past."

He sees an NWA patrol pass by, and a terrifying chill runs up his spine. He quickly asks, "Are they turning around?"

She looks into the rearview mirror, and hesitates for a moment and nervously says, "Maybe."

Jonathan confusingly responds, "Maybe?"

"No they kept going," she says. Then she smiles at him.

Some of the patrol vehicles have chip finders, and if they follow behind the car at a steady pace for 30 seconds, they can get an accurate reading to determine whether or not the driver in the car has a Bio chip. If they detect the driver is chipless, then they'll shot the vehicle with an Electromagnetic round to stop it. They also have drone patrols that use state of the art facial recognition software to locate people.

All these dramatic changes to society seemed to happen so fast and caught almost everyone off guard.

After the disasters hit, and the economies collapsed, they were forced to choose a lucid side. It was either spiritual freedom and environment, or industry and enslavement.

Jonathan was used to the freedoms he experienced before the collapse, under the amendments of the constitution. Like freedom of religion, career, travel, speech, but that was all long gone. Now freedom has a different definition.

It's freedom from enslavement and oppression. Eerily similar to the time when the Egyptians enslaved the Israelites and Moses freed them. Ronni surprisingly says, "You're kind of like the new Moses, here to free your people."

He semi jokingly says, "I guess it's about time for me to start performing some miracles," Ronni smiles.

Then Jonathan starts speaking like he is giving a lecture, "There's really another underlying conflict going on here... Between The God of the Universe, who created the Solar system, the natural Earth with its complex Eco structure, humans, and virtuous morals; Against the God of this World, with his unnatural concrete and steel creations, industrial petroleum technology, and perverted morals. They're battling for control of the Earth, because it seems to be very important to the universal power structure. Hypersensitive people can feel the different persuasive influences, and understand which side they're on. But some decent people were confused and have unknowingly combined elements of both God's, and wonder why bad things happen to them." He reflects for a moment, and then continues, "There was a time when the two worlds, natural and industrial, seem to co-exist. Good moral people thought they were living according to the righteous God's will, but they misinterpreted some of the crucial scriptures.

You see, When Satan tempted Jesus with the "World and all its glory," the ancient Roman civilization was at its height, and was controlling the known world at that period in time.

It was very similar to the economical, political, and social structure, including the sexual and religious freedoms, practiced by United States, before the collapse happened. That's the type of world Satan rules, and was offering Jesus."

They also seem to have misunderstood the scriptures when Jesus said, "If you want to be perfect, sell all your material possessions and give your money to the poor," and "It's harder for a rich man to get through the eye of a needle than it is for a rich man to get into heaven. And we can't disregard it when he also said, "You can't serve mammon and God. He was basically saying don't get emotionally attached to money and the material world, because that is not his kingdom...So people were thinking the material possessions they've acquired are blessings, when actually there a curse, imprisoning their soul to the physical world. They eventually get violently possessive when protecting their precious belongings and become targets of demonic attacks."

Ronni curiously asks, "What does it mean when someone is demonized?"

Then Jonathan profoundly says, "That's when someone embraces a sinful activity...You see, Satan's biggest trick was making people believe the truth is a lie, and the lie is the truth."

Ronni replies, "That is some heavy shit!" And then curiously asks, "How come the Universal God just won't come down here, right now, and just get rid of the Evil God that's causing the confusion?"

Jonathan, a little surprised replies, "I used to get frustrated by that same question, and I'm not really sure...But there seems to be events that must run their course, and lessons must be learned, before he can physically come back and defeat the Worldly God and his followers...But according to the prophecy he will, and I hope it happens soon!"

Ronni spiritedly replies, "Amen Reverend!"

Jonathan smiles and remembers his colleague Jeremiah, when he was trying to warn the

World about the devastating events that were coming.

He tried to inform them about how they could prevent them from happening by addressing the pollution problem. Governments could have stopped using fossil fuels and switched over to renewable energies and bio-degradable products. But they didn't listen, and that time, regrettable, has passed.

Jonathan thinks to himself, "God is punishing mankind because of their capitalistic greed, disregard for the Earth, and sexually perverted insolence."

He believes these types of practices, including the Gay and transgender activities, are a disrespectful slap to God's face.

Just like it is wrong for brother and sister to engage in sexual relationships. The same rule applies to men with men, and women with women. The gays try to confuse people with their modern intellect and say, "Because they love each other that makes it okay to practice sexual perversion."

That's not the kind of love that Jesus taught and preached. These sinful practices are very similar to the ancient Roman civilization, and are *not God's way!*

C7

They arrive at Granby Lake right while the sun is setting, and it briefly reminds him about Janae and their nature hikes.

Jonathan says, "Let's find a table in the picnic area."

She slowly pulls in and notices the picnic area is empty, and says, "Is this normal?" Assuredly he replies, "Yes, people usually don't come here during winter time."

They park the car by a table, get out of the car and sit down. They watch the sunset together, and take the time during their struggle to appreciate the beauty of God's creation in motion.

Jonathan sentimentally says, "I especially like sunsets during winter time, because that's when you get those orangey, reddish, blue colored skies.

It's like a work of art...Absolutely beautiful!"
They share a comfortable moment of silence as
they gaze at the natural beauty.

Ronni trying to be intellectual says, "I do see
proof of a creator. It's obvious in the
complicated structure of humans, and in the
elaborate ecosystem. But I also believe in
karma and reaching a spiritual level of Nirvana."
"Christians believe that you reap what you sow,
which is similar to the karma theory...And they
believe in a higher level of consciousness, which
is just like Nirvana." Jonathan quickly replied.
Ronni appreciatively says, "Don't get me wrong,
I truly believe in the Creator and what you've
taught me about the sacred way of the wise as
being a very important guideline to live your life
by. But what do you mean about you reap what
you sow? "
"Well, that's when you have to face the
consequences of your actions, good or bad."
said Jonathan.

Back at the house, Jimmy is working on the
route they're going to use to get to L.A. Miguel

and Keshaun are engaging in a discussion about religion.

Keshaun curiously asks, "Why was Mohammed able to unite all the Persian people?"

Miguel enthusiastically replies, "Did you know that Mohammed started the Islamic religion 700 years after Christianity was established, and the principles and morals in the Koran are very similar to the Bible?"

"I know Mohammed was visited by the Angel Gabriel in the cave" Keshaun defensively said.

Miguel amusingly answers, "Did you know that Gabriel is an archangel in the Old Testament of the Bible? You see, Mohammed was a tribal Hashemite clansman, and his people were fighting and killing each other over pagan gods and beliefs. He used to trade with the Christians and Jews on the road to Mecca. That's when he learned about uniting your people under one God, and how it can bring them peace...that's the revelation he experienced in the cave, and then created Allah and Islam. It is extremely similar to the story of Jehovah and Jesus."

A lot of the morals and principles in the Koran are the same as in the Bible.

Keshaun says, "That's a very interesting piece of the puzzle. I didn't know that...I hope Jonah is okay."

Jonathan and Ronni watch as Steven quickly pulls into the picnic area like he's running away from something bad. He skids into the picnic site where they're anxiously waiting. They rarely use phones to communicate because you can easily be tracked. There is voice recognition software called "Pegasus" integrated into the wireless phone network. Once the system makes an audio voice match, then it can lock onto your transmission, and locate your position. That's why they usually communicate using encrypted emails.

Steven gets out of the car and hurriedly approaches them and excitingly says, "Hey Jonathan, it's really good to see you!" Then he fearfully looks at the sky and says, "I think a drone was following me, but I lost it."

Jonathan refreshingly says, "It's good to see you too, my friend."

He joyfully hugs him and says, "You look a little paranoid."

"We live in a dark and dangerous time my friend." Steven nervously responds.

Steven comes from a loving, but strict upbringing. His parents were successful professionals and deeply cared about the well being of their son. They made him study day and night so he could succeed, and live a fulfilling life. His mother was Chinese and his father was French.

   Right after he graduated college, with honors at the age of twenty, his parents died in a horrific car accident while they were vacationing in The French Alps. This tragedy crushed him emotionally, and sent him on a journey to discover the meaning to life.

He wanted to know if God truly exist or not, and find tangible proof. But before he could figure out life's big mystery, the collapse happened.

He frustratingly says, "I really regret accepting this Bio-Chip, and working sucked before, but now it really sucks!"

He starts scratching his arm and continues, "Everybody is extremely unhappy. They micro-manage your every move, there is absolutely no privacy, and this scar itches." He has a triangle shaped scar on his forehand, which looks more like a cattle brand. When they inject the microchip into the middle of the wrist it leaves that triangle scar.

Ronni disapprovingly says, "That's the Mark of the Beast" everyone goes quiet.

Jonathan changes the subject and asks, "So have you found proof that God exists?"

"As a matter of fact, I have my good friend." Steven pauses and then boastfully replies, "I'm proof that Gods exist! I've come to the conclusion that I was created by a sophisticated intelligent being, who utilizes a fascinating evolutionary process to create human beings from an embryo...I had an epiphany and realized how complex the human body is;

from the skeletal structure, to the muscular design. Then you have the respiratory, cardio vascular and organ functions.

And let's not forget about the fascinating brain and nervous system...It's all so mind boggling complicated, that once I recognized this fact, that I was created by design and not by accident, it became my proof of a Creator! It's like how they have proof that Da Vinci existed because of his writings, inventions, and works of art...Well, I'm the Creators work of art!"

Ronni excitingly responds, "Yes! I know what you mean.

Jonathan is surprised and says, "That's a very interesting perspective; Well, It seems that you have completed your quest, my friend."

He affectionately pats him on the back and says, "Okay, show me what you got?"

Steven enthusiastically replies, "I got you the access codes, a key to the mainframe room next to the studio, and a layout of the facility...On December 13th, management will be gone for the day, attending an offsite function. There will be a window of opportunity for you to sneak into the main broadcast studio. We will have an hour to do a live broadcast of your message, and transmit it worldwide. If I try to upload a prerecorded speech, there's a good possibility it will be intercepted, and I don't want to risk it."

"Okay, I understand" Jonathan replied.

Ronni says, "Are you going to meet us at the entrance?"

"I won't be able too, because I'm going to be executing a strategically planned diversion...I'm gonna call in a bomb threat. Then everyone will have to evacuate the building."

Ronni sarcastically says, "That's your strategic diversion?"

"I know it sounds a little bit cliché, but it will work! It will take an hour for the bomb squad to arrive and start searching the building." Steven answered and then continues, "That's why I'm giving you the codes, key, and layout.

You must arrive at the exact coordinated date and time, enter the facility, and find your way to the main broadcast studio. Then hide in the mainframe room next to it by 3pm.

When the building is emptied, go into the studio and wait for me. If you are not in the studio by the time I get up there to operate the equipment, I'll assume there were complications, and the mission has been canceled for whatever reason. Do not try to communicate with me."

Jonathan replies, "Okay. Excellent my friend, what's the date?"

Steven starts feeling doubts about doing it, and reluctantly says, "Thursday, December 13."

He continues to feel doubt, but it suddenly passes and says, "I've got to get going; hopefully I'll see you then."

Jonathan spiritedly says, "Okay, but let me say a little prayer before you go," they huddle together, "Lord, we ask for your divine protection and guidance in these desperate and dangerous times. Amen."

Steve and Ronni reply, "Amen!"

He gives Jonathan, and then Ronni a long firm hug. This might be the last time they see each other.

They all get into their cars and quickly leave the lake in opposite directions.

Ronni concerningly says "do you think you can trust him?"

"I hope so! We just need to have a little faith." He reassuredly replied.

Jonathan and Ronni are now about an hour away from the safe house when a patrol vehicle pulls up behind them. The enforcers drive armored Humvees with all the latest surveillance and apprehensive technologies. Jonathan believes this one has a chip locator and thinks they're being followed and scanned. Jonathan seriously says, "As soon as they find out there's no one in the car with a Bio-Chip, they will attempt to pull us over, and if we do not comply, they'll shot an EM round at the car to stop us from escaping.

Ronni scaredly says, "I know they're going to try to pull us over, I know it, I just know It." And then she starts to panic and says, "What do you want me to do?"

Jonathan says, "Okay, keep your cool, let me think." He thinks for a moment and then says, "We'll wait till they hit us with an EM round, and when the car stops, will both get out and make a run for it."

Ronni surprisingly says, "What? That's it!?"

Jonathan with a serious tone continues, "We have to run in opposite directions to have a better chance of escape...I'll take the info packet, and we'll meet back at the house, if you get caught, you'll have three days to hold out before they force you to decide. That will give us a chance to come up with a plan to help you escape and vice versa." There is a moment of silence. The patrol car turns on the siren and flashes its lights.

Ronni excitingly says, "Oh Shit! Here we go!" She does not stop driving the vehicle, the enforcer gets on the PA system and angrily says, "Pull over now or we will be forced to stop you." Their adrenaline starts to kick in, and their hearts are racing like humming birds.

Ronni screams out the window, "We Live Strong and Die Free you heartless perverts!" They do not comply. Then they can hear the explosive sound of a weapon firing, and then a loud thud as the EM round hits the car, and it stops them in their tracks.

They swiftly jump out of the car like gazelles running from a cheetah, and a foot pursuit entails. Jonathan used to be on the track team, and Ronni is an ex-gymnast, so their chances of escape are very good. The enforcers are weighted down with armor and gear, so it's going to be difficult for the enforcers to catch them...But Ronni sees them chasing Jonathan. She quickly decides to fall and scream, like she injured herself, to get the enforcer's attention so they will come after her instead, and allow Jonathan to get away with the highly classified info packet.

C8

A NWA patrol vehicle is pulling up to the gate of the Colorado conversion center in Fort Collins. In the back seat sits a disgruntled detainee. The vehicle pulls up to the intake building and stops, the door slowly opens and an enforcer steps out, followed by Ronni from the "NEL."

They walk towards the door that leads to the processing center, and as they enter, there's a tall, large, butch looking women, with various steel piercings on different parts of her face. She has short, black, spiked hair and a very unpleasant facial expression as she looks at Ronni. She wears an obtrusive badge with the name Brenda Kujo on it. She says, with a serious tone, "Look what we have here! It seems that you have found yourself a pretty little stray, officer."

She asks Ronni, "What's your name, sweetheart?" Ronni doesn't respond. "Okay...What name should I call you?" she sizes her up and says, "How about Lil stray kitty cat." And then chillingly laughs.

Ronni stares intensely into her eyes and says, "How about Lil stray fist up your ass, tuna breathe."
Brenda slaps her, sand then forcibly takes her fingerprints and DNA sample.
Brenda angrily says, "Throw her into a holding cell!"
The enforcer briskly walks her to the holding cell, pushes her in, closes and locks the door.

In the cell, there are two other female detainees. Ronni flashes the NEL hand sign; that means holding up your thumb, index, and middle finger, which represents the spiritual trinity. But the two other detainees do not respond back. They just sit there with a look of fear and terror on their faces.

You can hear a high pitched scream coming from the other cell. Ronni asks the other girls,"whats happening?"
One of the detained girls scaredly answers, "It's probably one of the other girls getting raped by a guard. It's common here." Ronni asks them, "Have you've guys been raped?" Neither one of them answer." What's your name?" The cute petite white girl says, "Jasmine, and this is my friend, Megan"
"My name is Ronni, and I'm with the NEL," she proudly replied.
She can hear a low level voice coming out of the ceiling speaker, like a haunting entity, and it keeps repeating the words, "Renounce your God and submit to the will of the NWA."
She thinks to herself, "This is an institutional nightmare and I have to get the fuck out of here."
But then she remembers what Jonathan said about, "having three days before she's forced to make the crucial decision."

She hopes the rest of the crew is going to come up with a plan to help her escape before it's too late. The electronic lock disengages, the door opens, and an overweight middle aged guard enters the cell.

He has a disgustingly perverted look on his face as he checks out the girls.
The girls get this overwhelming creepy feeling, he grotesquely smiles at them and then leaves. The guard, Sgt. Nick Pervece, heads up to the captains office. He knocks on the door that says Capt. Willard on the name plate. He says, "Come in" the Sgt. enters and says, "Here's the list of the new detainees and when they arrived."

Capt. Mark Willard, a stern looking seasoned veteran, who is the nephew of General Pacstabus, cold heartedly replies, "How many executions are scheduled for tomorrow?" Sgt. excitingly responds, "Seven."

Back at NEL safe house, Miguel and Keshaun are engaged in a discussion about the mysterious book of revelations.

Miguel preachingly says, "Did you know that there are three critical phases of tribulations." Keshaun confusingly asks "What do mean?" Miguel answers, "Well...there are the seven seals, and then the seven trumpets, and then finally the seven bowls."
Keshaun curiously replies, "Okay, What about the four horsemen everyone talks about?"
Miguel excitingly responds, "Well, actually the Four Horseman are the first four seals."
He gets up from the couch and passionately continues, "The first seal is the white horseman; He who sits on this horse yields a powerful sword, and he will set out to conquer, and will conquer"
Keshaun still curious asks, "Who was that?"
Miguel sadly answers, "That was Hitler, who was an antichrist."
Keshaun with a tone of uncertainty asks, "What do you mean? Was he the Antichrist?"

Miguel slightly amused responds, "No, he was just one of many anti-Christ throughout time...You see, each horseman was a great tribulation that was unleashed on the world. The color of the horse is symbolic of the horrifying event that occurred. In this case, the color white represents the Arian's that Hitler claimed was the superior race. He spread fear and his message of hate that terrified mankind for years. And he conquered most of Europe, and almost the entire world"

Keshaun surprised says, "WOW! Okay that makes sense. What about the Red one?"

Miguel confidently replies,

"The second seal was the red horseman; He who sits on this horse will take peace from the Earth. Red was a symbolic color for the communist movement that kept the world in fear for some time, and almost escalated into a nuclear war. This tribulation happened right after the white horseman, which was WWII."

Keshaun is extremely impressed and says, "You are one *BAD ASS* homeboy, being able to figure that shit out...Well, what about the Black one?

Miguel amusingly says, "And he who sat on this horse held a balanced scale in his hand, stating, "This, is what's fair...I think you would know this one, My Brother."

They have an unspoken moment of understanding about the Civil Rights movement and racism.

Keshaun says, "Okay homey, I see. You're breaking it down. Now, what about the Pale Horseman? I'm guessing he was the third seal."

Miguel thinks for a moment, and then regretfully says, "Well, that horseman, who brought fear and death with him, was your radical Muslim buddies, The Islamic Terrorist."

Keshaun amazed replies, "Damn!... It's like this is a play by play list of events."

Miguel surprised responds, "Yeah, I think your right."

There's a loud crash and Jonathan runs in through the back door. He's exhausted and out of breath, and says, "They tried to pull us over, but we didn't stop, so they blasted us with EM. Then we had to make a run for it." He takes a couple deep breathes, "I need some water," quickly drinks, "did Ronni make it back?"

C9

Ronni and the other girls are anxiously sitting in the holding cell Ronni directly asks, "Are you guys gonna take the Bio-Chip?" The girls give her an indecisive shrug, and she continues, "Do *NOT* take it...because if you do, then you won't be allowed in The Eternal Kingdom."

"What do you mean, The Kingdom?" Jasmine intriguing asked.

Ronni enthusiastically continues, "It's the eternal Nirvanic Paradise! This life is all about proving whether or not you're worthy to enter." Jasmine listens as though she is being hypnotized. Ronni enthusiastically continues, "Once you are proven, you become enlightened, and when your fleshly body dies your resurrected and transformed into your eternal spiritual body of illumination, that exists in a euphoric suspended state of consciousness.

You will then have the ability to travel through universal space and time, and explore the infinite galaxies."

Jasmine curiously asks, "Really, how do you become proven?"

Ronni seriously replies, "You have to learn the sacred ways of the wise, and then you must be tested on that wisdom. If you pass, then you become proven."

"Can you teach me the way of the wise?" Jasmine hopefully asks, "No, but I know someone who can" Ronni answers.

Back at the safe house, Jonathan is talking to Miguel and Keshaun, "I have an overwhelming feeling Ronni was captured." He takes a moment as if he's trying to sense whether or not it's true.

Jonathan says, "If she's not here by morning, we'll need to figure out a way to break her out." He thinks for a moment and says, "She'll be at the Fort Collins Center."

Keshaun cooperatively says, "Okay Jonah, just let us know what you want to do."
Jonathan starts to yawn and says, "I need to get some sleep."
He goes into the bedroom. Keshaun then asks Miguel,
"How did you figure out those prophecies?"
Miguel with a tone of slight surrender reveals, "Well actually, I got it from a prophetic writer named Jeremiah. Back in 2020, he revealed the correct meaning of the Four Horseman, and was trying to warn the world about the coming trumpet tribulations in his book, 20/20 Vision."
Keshaun recollecting says, "Yeah I kinda remember hearing about him." There's a brief silence and then he asks, "What happened to him?"
Miguel hesitantly answers, "I'm not sure, but right after his book became successful, and before the disasters happened, he just disappeared.
Some say, Jeremiah and his people were raptured up into the sky."

And with an amazed tone says, "The chain of events he wrote about in his book actually came true!"

Keshaun inquisitively asks, "Was he some kind of biblical scholar?"

"No, He was an environmental scientist who converted to Christianity and became a writer," Miguel responded.

Keshaun trying to understand asks, "What were the plagues of the trumpets he warned everyone about?"

Miguel passionately answers, "Well the first trumpet was, a third of the Earth is scorched, which was the wild fires; the second was, a third of the sea life dies, which was caused from the sea level rising; the third was, a third of the fresh water is poisoned, which was from pollution and the forth was, a third of the sky is blocked from the Sun, which was the volcano eruptions."

Keshaun amazed, responds, "Damn, those were the same kind of disasters that caused the food problems, and the meltdown."

Miguel agreeing replies, "Si mon. And he also warned us about the two beasts rising, one from the sea and one from the land."

Keshaun surprisingly says, "The Serpent and The Dragon!"

Miguel adds, "Yes, Russia and China." And then he continues, "Let him who understands these words to be blessed with wisdom and insight."

Back at the center, Ronni is nervously pacing in the holding cell. Her adrenaline is pumping as she tries to figure out what to do. Jasmine and the other girl have fallen asleep. Ronni stops pacing, and an expression of realization appears on her face.

She hurriedly wakes up Jasmine and says, "I got a plan to get us out of here." Jasmine, half asleep rubbing her eyes, asks, "Really....What's your plan?"

Ronni excitingly explains, "Okay, here it is; I'll wait till the guard tries to rape me, I'll resist a little, but then I'll start to submit...Then I'll tell him to eat my pussy, and when he puts his head between my legs, I'll choke that pervert until he passes out. I'll grab his keys and weapon, then head out the front door and make a run for it." Ronni has extremely muscular legs because of her gymnastic training, and will have no problem chocking someone.

Jasmine sarcastically replies, "That's your plan? What about the guards outside?"
Ronni causally says, "Well, I hoping for a little bit of spirit magic to help me out with that...When do you think the guard will try and rape me?"
Jasmine unpleasantly says, "They usually come late at night"
Ronni settles down, and the girls try to fall back asleep.

Jonathan suddenly wakes up from an emotionally charged dream about Ronni running out of the gates of hell.
Frantically he wakes up the other crew members and says, "Ronni got caught! But she's going to escape from the conversion center. We need to get down there to pick her up."

Jimmy asks, "Did she call yet?"

Jonathan answers, "No, I had a vivid dream about her"

Jimmy adds, "Oh, I see, a spirit message."

  Jonathan smiles a little, and then says, "This will be a three-man operation, and were going to take the horses, because we need to stay off the roads, and the horses have night vision...There's hardly anyone driving on the roads at this hour, except for enforcers, and we don't want to risk losing another EV." He thinks for a minute, and then continues, "Jimmy, Keshaun and I will go, Miguel, you stay here in case Ronni shows up...and bring a couple of sticks of dynamite."

"Aye Aye Chief," Jimmy replies, "I'll get the horses ready."

All of a sudden, the satellite phone rings and everyone quickly stops what they're doing, and concerningly looks at Jonathan.

The Sat phone is what the underground high ranking officials from the American and European leaders use to relay encrypted communications with each other.

Jonathan answers the phone, and it's Martin Adams of the EuroResistance, he's Irish, and his family is related to some of the ex-IRA resistance leaders, like Michael Collins who fought during the English conflict, and seriously says, "We're going to cut off the head of the Snake!"

Jonathan unnervingly replies, "I understand, when?"

Martin continues, "As the sun rises, be ready for a solar storm" He hangs up the phone.

There's a very serious and distraught look on Jonathan's face.

Miguel nervously asks, "What's going down, Carnal?"

Jonathan reluctantly replies, "They're going to try and assassinate the Russian Dictator tomorrow in England when he arrives for a meeting with the Monarch of England."

The crew takes a moment as they wrap their heads around the information just relayed to them. Jonathan changes the subject and says, "Okay guys, we can't let that distract us right now, we've got to get going."

A couple of hours later, back in the holding cell, there's a clicking sound of the lock turning, and the door slowly open's.
Ronni wakes up expecting to see a guard, but it's Brenda the processing clerk.
Its right before dawn and the horseback crew is about a mile away from the center.

Ronni's laying on her side pretending to be asleep, Brenda creeps up right next to her and starts erotically stroking her leg and says, "wake up little kitty cat."
Ronni turns on her back and opens her legs, Brenda continues, "That's a good little pussycat, now I'll give you a treat."
Her head goes into Ronni's crotch.

Ronni immediately locks her legs around her neck and starts choking her, and then say's, "My God doesn't like sexual perverts. He takes it as an insult." Brenda's struggling to get up on her feet with Ronni around her neck. She spins around and tries to slam her into the wall to knock Ronni loose. But that doesn't work; she struggles for a little while longer but runs out of oxygen and collapse's. Ronni grabs her keys and baton, and then with a hopeful tone asks Jasmine, "Are you going with me?"
Jasmine scaredly replies, "What about the guards outside? There just gonna shoot us!"
Ronni encouragingly says, "You just got to have a little faith."

Jasmine reluctantly decides to go, but the other girl is way too scared to do anything. Ronni unlocks the door sticks her head out and waits till the coast is clear, and then says, "Let's go for it, Live Strong and Die Free."

They run out the door. They make their way down the hall, and since it's the graveyard shift there are fewer guards on duty, then they head out the front doors.

   Outside, the crew has just arrived at the center on their horses like heroic Cowboys of the old west. They're looking at the guard station and the gate, wondering what to do...Ronni and Jasmine look around and then start running for the gate. Jonathan can see the girls running and tells Jimmy, "Ride to the other side of the station, and toss a stick at the fence." Jimmy rides hard and get's close to the fence and stops, lights the dynamite, throws it and blows a huge hole in the fence. The guards aggressively run out of the station towards the fence. The explosion startled and surprised the girls, but they continue anxiously running towards the main gate. Jonathan blows a loud whistling sound that Ronni easily recognized. She excitingly says to Jasmine, "You see, It's Spirit Magic!"

One of the guards turns and sees the girls running out of the gate and shouts, "Stop, or we will shoot!" They continue running, and a shot is fired. Jasmine immediately drops to the ground.

Ronni turns around and sees her on the ground, stops, and runs back to her. Jonathan whistles again.

Ronni is all amped up on adrenaline as she knells down besides Jasmine, and notices she has a fatal wound, then asks, "Can you get up?" she replies, "Sorry I can't run anymore," she starts to cry. Another shot is fired, and she can hear the bullet buzzing by. The guards are running towards them.

Ronni tries to carry her, but can't. She knows, if she doesn't leave, she will probably get shot too.

Jasmine sadly looks at her and asks, "Did I pass the test?"

Ronni has an emotional moment of sadness, and then comfortingly says, "Yes, you did Jaz.

The Kingdom awaits your arrival" Jaz looks at her with a joyful look on her face and says, "How did you know that was my nickname?" Then she quickly dies.

Jimmy throws another stick at the guard station, and blows it sky high, and the guards stop shooting.

Ronni gets up, and sprints towards Jonathan and the others, she hopped on the back Keshaun's horse, and they quickly ride off right before dawn.

C10

The sun rises like a fiery skull peaking over the English horizon as it wakes another dreadful day in England. Today is when Dictator Demetri Butinov is scheduled to meet with the Monarch of England, William Ironside, at the Palace of Westminster to discuss crucial national security issues that will assist his efforts to eliminate the European underground.

Martin Adams is the leader of the European Resistance Army. He's going over the details of their plan, with his elite crew members, to assassinate the Dictator.

Martin is more aggressive with the battle against the NWA than the American underground, because he has a deep hatred for the Russians.

The Mafia kidnapped his daughter from a dance club in France when she was nineteen, and sold her to a high ranking Russian official who used her as a sex slave until she killed herself by overdosing on suboxones.

Martin used to be a Captain in the Army Ranger Wing of the Irish Defense Forces before the collapse, and would not submit to the Alliance.

He says to his crew. "Were going to have a once in a lifetime opportunity to erase this problem, so we have to make this count. Did you pick up the 3D printed gun?"

Seamus proudly answers, "I have it." He pulls an all white plastic .32 caliber pistol out of his jacket pocket.

Martin pleased says, "Okay good...I've been informed that before his meeting with the Monarch, the Dictator is scheduled to be interviewed on "The Charlie Michaels Show." This is the most watched talk show in the world. Everyone wants to be on this show. Over three Billion people tune in. The show broadcasts out of the BBC Studios in London.

Martin continues, "They will start taping the show at 10:00am (GMT), and that's when Charlie Michael's plans to present a lifelike statue of the Dictator, to the Dictator...the first part of the plan is to seal Seamus in a shipping crate, with the plastic gun, and have him delivered to the BBC Studio...the 3D Gun won't set off any metal detectors in the storage warehouse, so that the crate won't draw any attention."

James, the youngest crew member asks, "Who's going to deliver the crate?"

"One of my old ranger buddies that works for the Freight Delivery Service that handles the BBC shipments. He agreed to help us." Martin quickly replied, and then says to Seamus, "You'll arrive at the studio around 8:00am"

He pulls out a floor plan of the studio and points at the shipping dock, "Here's where they'll store the crate. You will have two hours to get out of the crate, and find the prop room.

When you get to the prop room, here," he points at a room on the drawing and says, "You should find the statue of the Dictator in there... When you do, get under the cover and hide on it, so when they wheel it out on stage and unveil it, you will jump out and slam a round into his head."

After a brief moment he sadly says, "There is no exit plan. This is a one way mission."

Everyone goes silent, Seamus, trying to lighten the mood with something funny replies, "Yeah... Well at least I'm gonna make a special guest appearance on The Charlie Michaels Show." Crew member James excitingly says, "Your gonna be *real famous* Mate! You'll definitely make it into the top ten greatest takedowns." Seamus shakes his head as to agree.

Martin concerning asks, "I want you to memorize the layout of the building."

He quickly answers, "Aye! Got it burned into my brain."

Martin continues, "If you succeed, you'll be delivering a major blow to one of the heads of the beast. This will be a great victory for the ERA."

That night they have a ceremonial feast similar to the last supper, and Seamus, is the sacrificial guest of honor.

The next morning arrives like a surreal moment in some history book. Seamus salutes Martin, and then he goes into the other room to put on his studio technician outfit and apply a fake scar on his forehead. He comes back out, and then walks towards the others. The crew members take turns giving Seamus a sentimental hug goodbye, knowing this will be the last time they'll ever see him. After that, he proudly says, "Live Strong and Die Free" then he slowly gets into the coffin like crate, and shuts the lid. It's equipped with a latch on the inside to easily open it. The delivery truck arrives as scheduled, and they ceremoniously load the fragile crate onto the truck.

They sadly, but proudly watch as the truck drives Seamus away into his heroic future.

Demetri Butinov has just arrived at the heavily guarded studio and is now getting prepared for the interview in his dressing room. He's sitting in a chair, staring at his reflection in the mirror, double checking his face for any irregularities. Then he recites his favorite Russian proverb, "Better to have a tomtit in your hand, then a crane in the sky" which means; "It's better to have a victory in reality, than it is to have an unreachable fantasy." The stage manager knocks on his door and says, "Sir, you're needed on the set in a half an hour," Demetri replies, "Da."

Jonathan and his crew have just arrived back at the house; they put the horses in the stable and go inside.

Miguel is watching the Alliance News Channel (ANC) and you can hear the announcer reporting a story.

"Recently there have been many unprovoked killer bee attacks on alliance citizens, and Entomologist are not sure why the attacks are happening. We advise people to either "Get to an enclosed shelter, such as a car or keep running until the bees stop following you." Jonathan, Keshaun, Jimmy and Ronni come walking through the door, and Miguel jumps up off the couch and excitingly says, "There's my bad ass home girl!" he gives her a passionate hug.

Back at the conversion center, Capt. Willard has just arrived, and his trying to find out how the detainee escaped. He's outside standing by the destroyed guard station.

Capt. angrily says, "How the Hell did this happen?"

Sgt. Pervece quickly replies, "Brenda was overtaken and subdued by the new detainee."

The Capt. suspiciously asks, "How did they get out of the holding cell to attack Brenda?"

Sgt. Pervece hesitates for a minute and responds, "They didn't get out before the attack."

The Capt. with a puzzled look says, "What do you mean?"

"Brenda was inside the holding cell when they attacked her" The Sgt. reluctantly replied.

Capt. Willard displeasingly shakes his head, knowing why she was in the holding cell and says, "Clean up this fucking mess, and get the pit ready for today's activities."

"The Pit" is what they call the area in the yard where they carry out the executions using a firing squad. Sgt. Pervece quickly replies, "Yes Sir!"

C11

Back at the BBC studios, the show is about to begin. The cameras are in position, the lights illuminate the celluloid set, and the band starts playing the song "Sympathy for the Devil" with a modern macabre spin.
Then at the end of the song, the highly energized announcer begins his symphonic introduction and proudly says, "Welcome friends and rivals to the Charlie Michaels Show."
The stage manager signals the smoke technician, the center of the stage fills with a thick layer of smoke, and then rising out of the floor, like a creature from the underworld, is the charismatic Host of the show. Then he says with a heavy English accent, "Hello, Hello, Hello Everybody!" the bands plays a measure from the Beatles song Hello/Goodbye,

"I don't know why you say goodbye I say Hello."
Charlie gestures, like he's irritated, for them to
cut the song. Then with a comedic tone, he says
his catch phrase, "What the Freak is going on
around here!"
The audience replies, "Who the Hell knows!"
They follow with applause.
Charlie continues, "Yes, Yes, Who does
know...Well, tonight I think we might just have
the right man who can tell us.
Our Supreme leader, Demetri Butinov, who will
be here momentarily" the audience applauds.
"But before he comes out, I would like to tell
you about a strange thing that happened to me
this morning when I was eating my curds and
whey...well along came this bloody spider that
walked up beside the edge of the plate. It was
black and red, and it looked at me, as if to say,
"Give me some of your whey" So, I said to it,
"Be on your way pesty spider," and right after I
said that, the little bugger started pumping up
and down like he was doing bloody pushups!

I was thinking, what the freak? Is this eight legged bloke trying to intimidate me? Well I didn't want him to bite me and turn me into some Spiderman super freak that would be crawling on walls, and shooting spider webs out of my ass! Sooooo...I gave him a piece of my biscuit, and he went on his way. I mean, What the Freak is going on?" He makes a quirky expression, the audience laughs, and then he says, "Well, it's time to introduce my first guest.

I would like to welcome to the show, the great, the powerful, and the most heartless Dictator everyone pretends to love... Demetri Butinov! So let's have a big unfriendly round of applause for my featured guest," the audience loudly claps.

The Dictator, who looks like Gorbachev on steroids, confidently walks out on stage and gives Charlie an, "I'm gonna get you back kind of look," and then he shakes his hand.
They smile at each other like their sharing a secret moment, and then they take their seats.

The audience stops applauding and Charlie says, "When did you realize that you wanted to grow up to be Dictator of the World?" and then with a heavy Russian accent, Demetri replies, "Well I guess it's when I was a young boy...we use to play a game called evil overlord."
Charlie surprisingly responds, "Evil Overlord?"
Demetri looks at him with a slight smile and continues, "All the children would hide, and if I found them, then I would rule over them for the rest of the day."
Charlie reacts with a quirky expression.

Demetri continues, "They would have to do anything I ask."
Charlie sarcastically responds, "Ahh Yes. That sounds like a lot of fun. I'm sure all the children loved it...Looks like I missed out on that fun experience" he gives another quirky expression.
Demetri responds, "Well Charlie, you can come over to my house sometime and I'll show you how to play."

Charlie sarcastically replies, "Well I'll definitely put that on the top of my list," he looks into the camera and continues, "Of things I *don't* want to do."

He gives another quirky look, the audience laughs, and then he says, "Well, just to show you our appreciation for being a good sport and coming on the show, we have a little present for you."

The stage techs roll out the covered statue. Seamus feeling excited and scared is waiting on the statue for his glorious moment.

They get ready to pull off the cover then Charlie says, "Wait," he asks the band, "Let me have a drum roll, please."

The drummer starts playing; they start to pull off the cover but it's sticking, so they pull harder, then it quickly comes off.

Seamus jumps off the statue, like a startled grasshopper, and runs feverishly towards the Dictator. Everyone on the set is surprised and a little confused, there not sure if this is part of the show.

Then Seamus suddenly stops, and for a moment it seems like everything is moving in slow motion as he points the 3D gun to his head, and fires a fatal shot. Demetri immediately drops to the floor as the warm blood starts to flow out of his head.

His personal body guards run out and start shooting at Seamus, a bullet hits him, he falls to the ground, they're still taping, and as the camera pulls in for a close up, and he says with his last dying breathe,

"This is Payback for the Pope you commie Wanker!"

He suddenly dies, and the screen fades to black.

C12

Back at the conversion center, it's a cloudy
overcast day; the mood is morbidly somber as
they prepare for the first execution. There are
two encouragement counselors in the
persuasion room trying aggressively to convert
a detainee who has been sleep deprived and
starved for three days.
The lead counselor with a very serious tone
says, "Your time is about to run out, are you
sure you want to put your faith in a God you've
never seen?" the weakened detainee doesn't
respond. The counselor still trying to convince
him says, "Don't waste your life taking a gamble
with a God that doesn't even exist...Do you
really think he's going to come down and
rescue you?" the detainee looks up and then he
continues, "I've seen your so called God let a lot
of his believers down...We are here on this

Earth by chance, by an accident in the Cosmo's... So this is your last chance. You just have to denounce your god and take the chip. And we will set you up with a job, car, and a place to live along with a monthly allotment of 2,000 credits."

The detainee has his head down like he's ready to capitulate and take the offer, the counselor presses on, "Come on, do you honestly think there's life after death?"

There's an uncomfortable silence, then the detainee slowly stands up. He shamelessly looks the counselor in the eye, and with a high degree of certitude says, "You bet your sorry, death kissing ass I do! Jesus rose from the dead, and so will I!"

The counselor frustratingly replies, "Okay, have it your way." Then he says to the guards, "Get this piece of shit out of here and take him to the pit, and watch him piss his pants." The guards violently grab him and take him out of the room. They walk the detainee down the hall of doom.

This is a hallway with pictures all over the walls of past victims and the gruesome method of execution they experienced.

All these people pissed the pants, and emotionally broke down at the last minute before they were brutally terminated. This hallway leads to the pit, where the execution pole and firing squad await their next victim.

The detainee tries not to look at the pictures as they slowly walk him down the hall. They arrive at the pit, and begin tying him to the pole. This is all becoming too real to the detainee now, as doubt starts to rise in him. Two shooters intimidatingly stand in front of him, thirty yards away. They cruelly delay for a moment, and wait to see if the detainee will break down. He struggles with an overwhelming emotional wave of fear and doubt. He's using every bit of his inner strength and will power not to give in. He wants to die with dignity. He starts speaking the words, "I believe it's true. Lord, give me the strength."

The guards slowly raise their guns and aim. All of a sudden, the detainee has a calm, peaceful feeling come over him, like all of his troubles have been lifted. Then a voice shouts, "Fire!"

Right before the guns explode and send their bullets to their target, it seems like time is moving in slow motion for a brief moment.... and then, "Bang!"
Next you can hear the chilling sound of lead, slamming into human flesh. Life quickly fades from the detainee, and then a guard heartlessly says, "Another rider for the Ferryman... Make sure to cut off his head because he was a Christian."

Back at the NEL house, the crew members are still celebrating Ronni's escape. You can hear them singing the song, "I Just Want to Celebrate" by Rare Earth playing in the background. Then Jonathan says, "I would like to make a toast to the creator for assisting us with a little bit of spirit magic, so we were able to successfully complete the escape."

They all raise their glasses, say "Amen" and take a drink of their wine.

They continue joyfully singing and dancing to the music. Jimmy goes into the living room to smoke some herb and relax. He's watching the ANC, waiting for a report about the assassination.

Miguel and Keshaun start talking about the trumpet prophecies again, and Keshaun asks, "Now, what was the fifth one?" Miguel looks at him like he's trying to remember, and then says, "That's where it talks about those creatures coming out of the bottomless pit and tormenting people who have taken the mark." Keshaun excitingly answers, "Yeah, that's the one."

There's a moment of silence, and then, like he's just figured out the meaning, he enthusiastically says, "What about the Killer Bee attacks?"

Miguel surprised says, "Damn homey, the spirit is moving in you today, I think you might have figured that one out."

Keshaun replies, "Actually... Jonathan told me about that one. Jeremiah went to the same college where he used to teach, and they use to have a lot of conversations about religion." Miguel responds, "Si mon."

They suddenly hear the words, "Breaking News" in the background. And with a pronounced tone the anchorman says, "Stay tuned for a Special Report"
Jimmy shouts, "Hey guys, you better get in here and listen to this!" The crew members eagerly gather around the television, and the anchorman continues, "This just in..."Demetri Butinov has been shot in the head by a member of the ERA while on the Charlie Michaels Show. The Dictator was rushed to the hospital for treatment, Stay tuned for any further developments."

There's an uncomfortable silence, and Joshua sadly says, "I predict that Demetri will make a miraculous recovery."
Miguel confusingly asks, "Why do you say that?"

Jonathan responds with biblical scripture; "And I saw one of his heads as it were mortally wounded; and his deadly wound was healed: and all the world wondered after the beast, as John of Patmos so elegantly wrote it."

Miguel amazed says, "Damn.... it's all coming true! Then he starts to get scared and says "this is too much to take!" he nervously paces around the room and continues, "Sometimes this shit just blows my fucking mind."

Jonathan, trying to calm him down concerningly says, "We should be rejoicing Miguel, because this means that the prophecies are true, and his glorious kingdom will come!" Miguel calms down and says, "Yeah you're right, we should be rejoicing. Glory and praise to the Creator and his first Begotten."

Back at the White House, Monarch Spade, General Pacstabus, and the other high ranking military officials, are in the situation room preparing for the extermination of the people in Mexoamerica.

Monarch Spade sternly asks, "Is the squadron prepped and ready for the mission?"

General Pacstabus quickly replies, "Yes sir! They'll start dropping their payload on the northern sections first, and then work their way down to the southern areas."

All of a sudden, the Monarch's special assistant urgently enters the room and hands him a note. He reads it, and with a very distraught look on his face, he tells the Generals, "The dictator has been mortally shot in the head."

The room is silent as they comprehend the news he just relayed. Monarch Spade continues, "We will not let this deter use from the mission that was approved by the Dictator. We will do this in his honor...Bring up the satellite feed for that territory."

The flat screen on the wall turns on, and now they're all looking at the targeted area. General Flynn, who's in charge of the Air force, concerningly says, "What about the innocent civilians?"

Monarch Spade gives him a look of dissatisfaction, and with a commanding tone says, "General, just give the order to launch the squadron."

General Pacstabus quickly gets on the Sat phone and calls the San Diego military base, and gives the green light command to launch the mission.

Down in the town of Chihuahua, a mother is feeding her 7 year old daughter some beans and rice. As she's cooking some tortillas on the hotplate, she hears men yelling and screaming. Then there's the sound of automatic gunfire, like a macabre drum roll.

She urgently says, "Bebe, vena qui y ponte en el piso" She runs over to her mother, and they both lay down on the floor. Then comfortingly she says, "Pase lo que pase recuerda que Mami te amo." Her daughter crying replies, "Yo tambien te amo Mama."

Shortly after that, they can hear the roaring sound of airplanes, like a giant swarm of hungry locust, getting louder and louder as the deadly squadron approaches its target.

Next, they hear the terrifying whistles, of bombs dropping. Soon the bombs will indiscriminately unleash their deadly gas, and suffocate the unsuspecting people in Mexoamerica.

The distraught mother passionately hugs her crying daughter, presumably she thinks, for the last time...Explosions ring out like a "symphony of destruction." Then you can hear screaming, like vocalist in a morbid opera, as they give their final performance, before death ushers them off the stage of life.

In the situation room, the highly classified audience is watching in amusement as the people in Mexoamerica take their last breaths. General Pacstabus cruelly says, "Bravo."

C13

Back at the NEL house, Jonathan's crew is finishing up their victory celebration for Ronni's escape, and trying to extend the moment for as long as possibly can, before they have to get some sleep and start planning for the pirate broadcast mission. Jonathan announces, "The spirit was with us on this last mission, and I hope it will be on this next one."
Everyone replies at the same time, "Amen!" and they all take a drink of their wine.

Then there's a loud banging on the front door, and everyone in the room goes quiet. The banging continues, and concern starts to rise in the room. Then someone outside anxiously says, "Miguel, are you in there? It's me Takoda, let me in."

Takoda is one of the local boys that Miguel has been shepherding, along with a couple of other ones. He has been teaching them the way of the wise, so they can become spiritually proven. Once there ready, they'll be able to assist with the resistance activities, and spread the message.

When Jonathan dedicated his life to God, he researched all the different religions to find the sacred way of the wise. The Christian bible was where he found most of the wisdom.
He thoroughly studied Judaism, to understand the Creators origin, and his complicated relationship with the chosen people.
Then he meticulously studied The New Testaments so he could better understand the modifications made to Judaism that became Christianity. Jonathan figured out how to align and synchronize himself with The Eternal Creator so he could feel the peace and joy of the Holy Spirit. Miguel goes to the door and looks out the peep hole, looks back at Jonathan and nods, and then opens the door.

Takoda urgently enters, and then Miguel firmly says, "Haven't I told you not to show up without being summonsed."
One of the spiritual tests is Loyalty. You must keep your word when given to another brother. Takoda nervously replies, "I'm Sorry, my brother, but this is very important."
Miguel, a little bit irritated says, "Okay, I'll give you grace on this one, but don't let it happen again... What's going on?"
"The governor is allowing deforestation in our area. I just saw the convoy of heavy equipment coming through the town." Takoda replied. Colorado already has the Bark Beetle problem with the trees because of climate change, so any deforestation induced by man is a very serious issue.

Jonathan thinks about the angel visitation when he was told to "Be Stewards of the Earth," and then he hears a single chirp from a cricket at the same time he's thinking about that, creating a moment of synchronicity that reassures him the reminder is from the spirit.

He remembers when he became aware of the living God. He began feeling a very strong connection to nature and the animals. Jonathan can understand some of the animals when they're communicating.

He thinks about the scripture of the "living creatures with wings," how they have "many eyes on their wings." That's when he realized it means that all the insects and animals are interconnected.

Jonathan eagerly asks Takoda, "Which way were they heading?" Takoda points north. "Okay guys, we need to come up with a quick plan to disable the equipment...Jimmy, get me a map of the local area" Jimmy gets the map, and gives it to him. He lays it out on the table. Jonathan pointing at the map continues, "So, they were heading up hwy 25 to hwy 70, probably going to Leadville." Jonathan contemplates for a moment and says, "Okay Takoda, are you ready to prove your courage and faith?"

Takoda quickly replies, "I'm ready to make my ancestor proud. Just let me know what you want me to do to prove that I'm worthy."

The first step to proving someone is worthy is to understand the meaning of the virtuous wisdom.

The second step is to have each virtue, embedded into the moral structure of their character by completing each individual test. Then you're "proven" for that specific attribute when you pass the test.

This process will establish what morals have become absolute within the soul of the individual. This testing process galvanizes the wisdom in your soul. When you pass all the tests, then you become "Spiritually Proven." This is the first of two phases.

The second is "Divinity." This is how someone can completely align their soul with the Eternal Creator.

The Holy Spirit that Jesus spoke about will help guide you through situations here on Earth in order to achieve "Complete Enlightenment."

The Nine sacred virtues or "The Way of the Wise" tests to become spiritually proven are;

Loyalty: To be a person that keeps their spoken word and stands by what they believe.

Courage: To remain unwavering during adverse endeavors, even when you become extremely terrified.

Faith: To believe and trust in a God, and what he wants you to do, even though you've never physically seen him.

Carry-out assigned tasks not knowing the outcome, and recognize the invisible power of the Holy Spirit when it's influencing a situation, and act on it.

Endurance: To persistently stay strong when the opposition tries to crush your beliefs and spirit. Keep a cool head when the situation gets heated.

Patience: To tolerate difficult situations without losing your temper, and getting violently upset.

Diligence: To continuously care for the one true God, and stick together, even through the difficult times.

Obedience: To carry out the will of the Eternal God; Learn and sustain the biblical morals and commandments, like, you should not murder, steal, commit adultery, bear false witness etc... And know the modifications that Jesus made to the laws. You should also be stewards of the natural Earth. Maintain balance and moderation in your life.

Sacrifice: To let go of something you cherish for the sake of the greater good, and put someone else's needs before your own. Selflessly risk your life for another member.

Respect: To exhibit sincere admiration and reverence to your chosen elders, and fellow brothers. Learn how to treat someone as if it was your own flesh.

The next level to achieve is Divinity. This occurs after you learn the divine attributes, which are;

Prudence: When you know how to judge someone accurately and accordingly. To learn that when you judge someone, you will be judge by the same measure based on their life experiences. You must be extremely careful, because if you're inaccurate, then the same infliction of punishment will come back on the judging individual.

Mercy: To know how to forgive someone. Develop the skill to recognize when someone is truly sincere and remorseful for their wrong doing. And if they are sincere, then you forgive them, but if there not, then you inflict proper punishment to prevent that person from becoming demonized.

To pass any test, you must be in the circumstance that requires you to exhibit that specific characteristic appropriate for the given situation. Once you have properly displayed the attribute in a real life situation, then you have passed the test.

Jonathan says to Miguel, "Do you think their ready to prove themselves?" Miguel respectfully nods yes. Jonathan continues, "Okay...Then were going to use them for this next mission."

There are four "Newgens" that Miguel is shepherding.

Newgens are the new generation of true believers. There is Takoda; who's a native Indian form the Apache tribe with archery and survival skills, Caleb; who is a semi-pro snowboarder, Shaun; is a stunt cyclist, and Marco, the intellectual musician.

The plan is to have them sneak into the worksite, distract the guards, and add sugar into the fuel tanks to disable all their heavy equipment.

They will utilize their stealth and distraction skills, combined with their natural talents. They should be a substantial force that will hopefully make a significant contribution to the movement.

Miguel walks over to Takoda and proudly says, "I need you to round up the tribe kemosabe, and bring them here tomorrow!" Takoda acknowledging with a nod quickly heads out the back door to round up his fellow tribesman.

C14

Back at the ERA safe house, Martin Adams and his team are having a spirited Irish style celebration after hearing the news about the Dictators assassination. They're toasting to the success of their brave and selfless mate, Seamus, who sacrificed his life for the cause of the underground movement.

Martin somberly says, "In this bittersweet moment, I would like to honor our mate," and then he lifts his glass and recites...

"Here's to a noble life and a merry one,
A quick death and an easy one,
A pretty girl and an honest one,
A cold pint...and another one!"

James quickly adds, "And may the good Lord open the gates for our fearless mate Seamus!" Everyone else responds, "Here, here."

They all drink a shot of Irish whiskey, and chase it with a tall cold glass of draught beer. They continue celebrating throughout the night with music and spirits. This helps them forget about their dreadful reality for a little while. But there's still a lingering sadness in the celebratory air, like a stormy cloud that looms over their heads.

Back at the California State Capitol Building, Ambassador Davidson, Governor Clovis and Governor Grayden of Colorado, are in the executive conference room talking about the assassination attempt, the vandalism at the stadium, and the escape at the Fort Collins Conversion facility. The other governors have gone back to their territories.

The Ambassador frustratingly says, "What the Fuck is going on around here?"
He hesitates like he's waiting for an answer, but then continues, "Our Battleball clubhouse was contemptuously vandalized, a possible high ranking NEL member escaped, and we can't

forget that the Dictator was fucking shot in the head... on the Charlie Michaels Show!"

There's an uncomfortable silence, and then Governor Grayden defensively replies, "But we did get a photo, fingerprints and a DNA sample from the escapee, so now she's in the system and will be easier to locate."

"I would hope so...let's find that little bitch, and get the name of their damn leader." Davidson firmly responds and then adds,

"Every day they live, they keep the myth of their God alive and give hope to the people. I mean; how can they be so stupid to actually believe God exists...There is no real proof, only fairy tales."

Governor Clovis then adds, "It is ridiculous, if you really think about it." He stands up and passionately continues, "It doesn't make any sense. To have this enormous power to create a complex universe, but he can't make the less intelligent humans, that he also supposedly created, do what he wants...And another odd thing is, he never shows himself."

Ambassador jokingly says, "Maybe he's scared of humans?" They start laughing hysterically.

Brian Cheeves has just arrived at the broadcast center to start his shift. He's the stage manager for the Alliance News Channel. He drives up to the gate, and the unpleasant looking guard, that he sees every day, asks him to swipe his hand under the scanner. And with very low enthusiasm, he complies.

The guard lets him pass, he drives onto the studio lot, parks his car, and he goes inside. He carries out his mundane duties to get the set ready for the morning news broadcast. He makes sure the lighting techs have done their jobs right, double checks the stage for furniture and props, makes sure the teleprompter is updated with the current dialogue, confirms the cameramen are in position, and then tells the anchorman that it's "thirty minutes until taping begins."

Brian's wife is at the house, beginning to experience a psychotic episode because she hasn't been taking her medication.

She hears a demonic voice, disguised as a voice of reason, convincingly telling her to, "Save herself and the children from the agony of this life, and send them to the afterlife, where they'll be happy and free from this horrifying world."

The demonic spirit is embedding itself deeper into her soul, and has a stronger influence on her personality.

Olivia stares at her children, with a semi spaced out expression on her face, as they play with their toys. Their son is playing a violent video called "Living Dead Zombies," and her daughter is playing with lifeless Barbie dolls. She goes into the bathroom and opens the medicine cabinet, and slowly reaches for her prescription bottle of OxyContin.

She grabs it as if this is the only remedy that will save them from the horror of alliance controlled life.

She takes a bottle into the kitchen. She thoroughly crushes up all the pills and mixes them into a container with fruit punch.

She carefully pours punch into three glasses, each filled with a lethal dose of medicine. She hesitantly stares at the deadly punch filled glasses, as she wrestles with the persuasive voice inside her head, and tries to decide whether or not to carry out her demented plan.

Back on the news set, Brian is just about to start the morning news broadcast; the anchorman is in his seat, he double checks his list of duties, and then gives the action signal. The anchorman says, "Our top story today; Crazed gunman goes on a terrifying shooting spree, and brutally killed 12 people at a local food distribution store...Iraqi Veteran Glenn Miller took an M-16 and went into the store and shot two guards, a grocery store clerk, and nineteen shoppers, before blowing himself up killing twenty more people. The store manager said, Mr. Miller was a regular patron at this location, but was upset when he ran out of credits, and was denied any food purchases." "Our Next story; the current number of Suicide victims have skyrocketed in the last year from

100,000 to a staggering 250,000 people, the highest amount ever recorded."

Brian starts to think about his wife for a brief moment, and then Steven Ferris, Jonathan's gracer friend, walks into the studio and urgently heads right towards Brian and tells him he's here to troubleshoot the malfunctioning software in the control room.

The anchorman continues with the newscast, "And now for a Special Report...Crow attacks have been on a rapid rise. They strategically attack in packs, and usually, try to eat their targeted victim's eyes out. They are showing signs of extreme intelligence, and only seem to attack people with the Bio Chip."

Back at the NEL house, Jonathan and the others are waiting for Takoda to round up the other Newgens, so they can send them on their first operation.

Miguel asks Jonathan, "How come the Jews were easily crushed by the Iranians and Russians if their "God's chosen people?"

Jonathan answers, "Well...It's because they're no longer his chosen people." Miguel confusingly responds, "What do you mean?" Jonathan continues, "They were his favorite for some time, before Christ came. But after they rejected Christ the Messiah, they were no longer his chosen ones."

Miguel intriguingly listens as Jonathan continues, "You see; Jesus fulfilled the prophecies, and performed the miracles that proved he was the Messiah...He died to free us from the curse of the law; because the law created sin, and sin brought death. So now we have the grace to correct our moral mistakes and get it right, and not to be eternally damned...But that doesn't mean you can continue to sin without any repercussions.

  You must continue to strive and strengthen your spirit by resisting sinful behavior. It's like how you strengthen your body muscles when you work out at a gym. If you don't believe what Jesus did is true, then you're still bound by the curse of the law...The Jews used to have to offer up an animal sacrifice to appease God, so they would receive his mercy and not get punished for their sins. But when their temple was destroyed by the Romans, they stopped the daily sacrifices."

Miguel asks, "So why do they think God would grant them grace, when they didn't accept Jesus as the Messiah, and they're no longer offering any animal sacrifices?"

Jonathan impressed with his question, answers, "Because of their misguided arrogance...But they did want to rebuild Solomon's temple to perform sacrifices, and so their Messiah would finally come."

Miguel adds, "Si Mon...So if you don't believe Jesus was the Messiah, then there is no grace, and your shit out of luck!"

Jonathan responds, "Amen! That's why they were scattered and persecuted for so many years...When God punished his people in the old time, he would allow barbarian army's, like the Philistines, Assyrians, and Babylonians to brutally conquer his chosen people when they were committing too many sins."

Miguel curiously asks, "Is that why groups of people still hate them today? Is God using those people to punish them?"

Jonathan sadly answers, "That's a very good possibility"

Miguel, a little confused asks, "But what about the Jews reforming the State of Israel?"

Jonathan quickly replies, "Well, that was just the accomplishment of their human willpower that allowed them to re-establish their state for a brief moment in time. And that made them falsely believe they were still the chosen ones."

Miguel replies, "I see what you mean, it makes sense." There's a drumming knock at the back door, Keshaun checks to see who's there, it's the Newgen's, so he lets them in.

These are the sons of some of the biggest Hollywood stars, before they fell from the celluloid sky.

They've been hiding in Colorado since the collapse happened, and have managed to avoid capture or being forced to take the Bio Chip. Now it's mandatory to accept the chip when you reach the age of thirteen.

The NWA aggressively went after any influential major talent; Movie directors, writers, actors, musicians and talk show personalities to silence their opposing opinions, and take away their ability to persuade anyone with their media skills.

They all could have united together and used their star power to address these critical social and environmental problems, but they more interested in making money and getting praises from their fans.

Most of them shamefully converted, and now are being censored and closely monitored.

There were some that just disappeared. Rumor has it, is that they're hiding out in underground facilities that were built in case nuclear war broke out.

Miguel's tribe members eagerly walk in, their average age is seventeen, and there full of youthful enthusiasm, waiting for the chance to prove themselves worthy.

They take turns fist bumping Miguel, and then he asks, "Are you guys ready for a little action? And contribute to the Holy Crusade?"

Shaun; a tall, skinny, redhead confidently replies, "I was born to Ride or Die!"

Caleb; a short, olive skinned, blonde haired boy chimes in. "Let's derail these Lame O's."

He slaps hands with Shaun, and then Marco; a large, strong, brown haired boy adds, "It's time to set this town on fire, and rock their world."

Takoda, the Native American kid, stays silent with an extremely serious look on his face.

Jonathan says, "That's the spirit...Okay guys gather around, and I'll break down your assignments for this operation."

He pulls out some pictures, "Jimmy did some recon, and shot these pictures of their camp and equipment. There are five guards, and ten workers...Miguel, you'll drive the truck, and take Shaun, Caleb, and Marco, along with their bikes, to the logging location...I want you guys to ride your bikes into the camp, and start doing your best BMX tricks to get their attention."

He looks at Marco and says, "Then Marco; you'll try to talk one of the guys into betting on a bike race between you three, putting up this 3oz gold nugget if he can guess the winner." He tosses him the nugget and says, "Don't lose it." Even though cash is worthless, solid gold is still worth its weight. You can turn it into credits, or use it to barter on the black market. Jonathan continues, "When they're all distracted because of the bike race, Takoda, I want you to sneak onto the dozers, and pour the sugar water into the gas tanks each one of them." Takoda asks, "What if the tanks are full?"

Jonathan casually replies, "You'll need to bring a siphon to get some of the gas out."

Takoda answers, "Okay, I know how to pick gas cap locks."

Jonathan impressed replies, "Cool! Your ancestors would be very proud of what you're doing. They truly understood the balance that must be kept between man and nature."He thinks for a moment, and then continues, "You and Jimmy will ride in on horseback and sneak into the camp...When Takoda has finished dowsing the fuel tanks, Jimmy will give you the signal to get out. When you hear his howling wolf call, Marco, I want you to point out the fact that there have been recent wolf attacks in the public camp area, so they'll check around their camp."

He points at Shaun, Caleb, and Marco and says, "Then you guys slip away, as soon as you can, and ride back to the truck where Miguel will be waiting."

Takoda replies "Cool."

Jonathan, slightly amused from his reply, continues, "The operation is set for tomorrow afternoon, at the end of the day around five pm, when there shutting down for the day."

C15

Back on the news set with Brian Cheeves. There almost at the end of the broadcast, his mind is preoccupied as he partially listens to the anchorman reporting about Ronni's escape, and posting her picture with a hotline phone number or what the underground refers to as the "ratline."

He's getting anxious and wants to get home to check on his family. Because ever since he heard the suicide report, he has been concerned about his wife. He tries to call, but there's no answer. He calls over his assistant and says," I have an emergency at home, and I gotta leave."

His assistant nods, and he frantically runs out the studio and rushes to his car, starts it, and races out of the parking lot, almost crashing into another car, as he dangerously speeds down the highway. He pulls into the driveway and runs up to the house, dreading what he might see. As he walks through the door, he hopes his deepest fear is not about to come true... then he sees his family lying on the floor. And with a painfully heart crushing scream yells, "Nooooo!"

He runs to her side and frantically shakes her, trying desperately to wake her up, with no success. He checks for a pulse but cannot find one.

He woefully cries for a moment, and then sits down beside his wife and takes her lifeless body in his arms. Then he starts gently rocking her back and forth and begins to softly sing her favorite song, "Broken Wings" by Mr. Mister. "Take, these broken wings, and learn to fly again, learn to live so free, and when we hear the voices sing, the book of love will open up for us and let us in."

Back in the Capitol State Building, Ambassador Davidison is engaged in a fervent phone conversation with Monarch Spade about the assassination attempt.

The Monarch is extremely upset and wants to increase security at all broadcast facilities, and escalate the efforts towards eliminating the underground.

Monarch Spade commandingly says, "I want you to cooperate and assist the ABI with their investigation, into the escape of the NEL detainee, at the Fort Collins Conversion facility."

The Ambassador cooperatively replies, "Yes Sir, I will dedicate all my resources and pursue this possible connection to the resistance leader...Do you think they are planning to assassinate you?"

Monarch replies, "The thought did cross my mind."

Ambassador concerningly asks, "Is Demetri going to pull through?"

"I don't know, but he's one tough Ruski," replied the Monarch.

"We're still waiting to hear back from the hospital. I'll let you know as soon as hear something."

Ambassador Davidson says, "Okay, I'll keep you informed about any new developments about the escape." He hangs up the phone and frustratingly looks at Governor Grayden and says, "Well, it looks like I'm going to be taking a little trip to Colorado, to meet up with the ABI agent in charge of the escaped detainee investigation."

Back at the NEL house, their getting ready to begin operation "derail the loggers." Miguel's Newgen tribe is scared, but excited to have the chance to move forward, so they can prove themselves worthy to enter the kingdom, and be a part of the underground movement.

Jonathan encouragingly says, "Okay guys, are you ready to do this?" They all acknowledging nod their heads, but you can sense a vibe of uncertainty in the room.
Miguel enthusiastically says to Shaun and Caleb, "Okay lil homies, get your bikes and put them in the back of the EV truck." Shaun spiritly replies, "No problemo O.G." and they head out the door.

Jimmy and Takoda head out to the stable and get the horses ready to ride. While there saddling the horses, Takoda asks Jimmy, "Do you really believe God exists?"
Jimmy replies, "Well I'm not 100% sure like Jonathan, but I do believe enough to take a chance that he does exist.

I do believe it's wrong to unjustly kill people, and to destroy the Earth. I've seen the affects of the Holy Spirit."
Takoda surprised with his honesty says, "My ancestors believed in "The Great Spirit," which I think there one and the same."

They look at each other and share a moment of understanding, and they continue preparing the horses.

Jonathan gives Miguel some last minute advice and tells him, "Remind your guys about how the spirit can work its magic in a situation, so they know what to look for."

Miguel respectfully answers, "Si mon Carnal!" and heads outside. There cautiously driving down the highway, trying not to draw any attention, as they head towards the logging camp. They arrive and stop a quarter mile before their target destination.

Shaun, Caleb, and Marco get their bikes out of the back of the truck and hesitantly get on them, but before they ride off Miguel says. "Hey guys, I have something I need to tell you. Remember to look for the influences of the Holy Spirit when it's trying to help your situation, like subtle signs and silent mental inspirations. "They nod their heads. "

And now I want to say a prayer," everyone bows their heads, and he continues,

"Lord, send the power of the Holy Spirit to assist these men with their task, and guide them as they prove their worth. Amen!"

They guys open their eyes, and Miguel asks, "Are there any questions?" no one does have any, and they slowly ride away to their targeted mark."

The crew at the logging site is shutting down for the day, as the boys ride in. The workers are surprised to see them and wonder what they're doing out here. They boys ride through an open lot and stop in front of the office trailers.

Adrenaline kicks in, and they feel like they just drank ten cups of coffee. There trying to stay calm as their hearts are racing like Eagles.

A couple of unpleasant looking armed guards approach them, and one of them asks, "What are you guys doing out here?"

Marco gets off his bike, walks over and says," Were just camping with our families and got bored. We wanted to see what's going on here."

The guard answers, "Nothing here that concerns you guys, so go back to your campsite."

Marco's getting nervous he will fail his task, and screw up the operation. He hesitates for a moment hoping to think of something to say. All of a sudden he feels a sensation of inspiration come over him, and then comes up with the Idea to say that he found the 3oz gold nugget.

He hears a crow caw, and then says, "Hey, check out this nugget I found over there in the stream...I think it might be gold?" The guard curiously walks over and looks at it. He gets on the radio and tells the supervisor, and he quickly comes out.

This older, rugged looking man, with a stern look on his face, comes out of the office trailer and walks over to them and says, "let me see this nugget."

Takes a look at it, and does a scratch test on a ceramic plate, and the nugget test's positive.

The supervisor curiously asks, "Where did you find this?"

At this point, Jimmy and Takoda have gotten into position and are waiting for the others to start the race and distract the workers enough to begin dowsing tanks.

Marco replies, "I found it in the stream over there," and he points at a wooded area south of their location."

The supervisor asks, "Can I keep this as a sample?"

Marco quickly replies, "No way, José!"

The supervisor eagerly asks, "What do you want for it?" Marco knows he's got him on the hook and says, "How about this; will make a race track in this open lot, and my bros will do 5 laps, and if you guess the winner, I'll give you the nugget, but if you guess wrong, then you get us four cases of red bull." Red bulls are a luxury beverage now, and are hard for the general public to purchase.

The Supervisor suspiciously replies, "But if I tell you my pick, you'll know who to let win."

Marco quickly responds, "Then write your pick down on a piece of paper, and stick it in this cup, and at the end of the race will see who you chose." The supervisor quickly agrees on the bet.

The workers make a track in the empty lot, as Shaun and Caleb get ready to race. Takoda sees the plan is working and starts dowsing the fuel tanks.

Everyone is gathered around the makeshift race track watching them warming up. The guys are doing a variety of BMX tricks on their bikes, megaspins, tailwhips and whiplash's while the other workers are making bets amongst each other, as the race is about to begin.

Takoda sneaks in like a panther approaching its prey, and climbs on the first bulldozer. He quietly moves over to the fuel tank and notices there's no lock on the cap, he turns and removes the cap, siphons some gas out, and pours in the sugar water, and then carefully replaces the cap.

He confidently says, "One down and six to
go." He jumps off the gigantic beastly machine
of destruction, and thinks to himself, "This is
much easier than he imagined."
As he's moving stealthily towards the next one,
he unexpectedly hears a gunshot blast, and
immediately stops in his tracks.

C16

Over in the Middle East, it's another hot, dry, and dreary day, with the unpleasant wind blowing a mixture of sand and dirt through the hostile air. There's a convoy of small trucks speeding down a grimly barren dirt road loaded with Muslim resistance fighters, and some much needed supplies. There heading for the hidden fort in the mountainous region of Afghanistan to plan for their next offensive. They no longer plan attacks against the great Satan that was formerly known as the U.S.A. and their allies, but now they inflict Jihadist terror on their own people. Waiting patiently at the cavernous hideout, is their fearless superior, the current architect of terror, Mustafa Rahman also is known as "Rahman the Great."

He and his army vigorously fight to maintain their belief in the prophet Mohammed and Allah. The Monarch of Iran and a majority of the Muslim population have betrayed them and renounced Allah, and pledged loyalty to the "NWA."

Rahman the Great has a simple but aggressive strategy to bring his people back to Islam. It's either reconvert or kill them.
He plans to begin with the local tribes, and then continue spreading outward throughout the Muslim regions, reconverting and growing his army as they continue advancing their Islamic holy campaign.
Just like his ancestor Abdul Rahman achieved in Europe during the 7th century.

Back at the logging site, the gunshot that Takoda heard was a guard firing his pistol to start the bike race. The workers and guards are excitingly cheering and yelling as the boys give them an entertaining spectacle to keep them distracted.

Takoda has just finished dowsing the fuel tank of the sixth dozer in the treacherous fleet of heavy equipment. He jumps down and cautiously heads for the last one, but he unexpectedly surprises a guard that has walked over to the monstrous bulldozer to relieve his bladder.

They curiously stare at each other for an uncomfortable moment, and the guard begins to wonder what he was doing on the dozer and then asks, "What are you doing here?" Takoda doesn't answer. Then he quickly turns and starts running as fast as he can back to the horses, and the guard follows close behind. The race is on its last lap when a loud explosion immediately gets everyone's attention. Shaun and Caleb skid their bikes to an abrupt stop. Jimmy has thrown a stick of dynamite to stop the guard from chasing Takoda, but accidently threw it to close to the dozer and blew it up.

The supervisor forcibly grabs Marco by the arm, and angrily says, "What the fuck is going on here?

Are you responsible for this bullshit?" Marco freezes from fear. His heart is racing and doesn't know what to do. Then he sees a half eaten apple on the table right next to them, and remembers what Miguel said about the subtle help from the Holy Spirit.

He instantly turns his head and bites the supervisors arm as hard as he can, the excruciating pain forces him to let go of Marco, and he desperately runs towards his bike. One of the workers starts to run after him, but Caleb rides up a make shift ramp, made from a pile of cut lumber, and does a phenomenal front flip flair trick and hits the worker in the back of the head, knocking him down to the unforgiving ground. Marco swiftly gets on his bike, and the three of them rapidly peddle their bikes out of the logging camp to find Miguel waiting at the entrance.

They immediately abandon their bikes, and quickly jump into the back of the truck, and Miguel speeds away, like a demon escaping the lake of fire.

Takoda has made it back to his horse, and they quickly ride off into a heavily wooded area and vanish. The guard is frantically running back from the area where Jimmy threw the dynamite.

He's practically out of breath and says, "They almost blew my ass to smithereens!"

The supervisor is applying pressure on his bitten arm and frustratingly screams, "Who's they? What the hell happened?"

"Well, I was taking a piss by the dozer, and this kid jumped off of it and takes off running like a startled deer...Then the dozer blew up!" The guard hysterically replied.

The astonished supervisor thinks about it for a minute, and tries to figure out what has just happened. He concludes that the guard accidentally flawed the "NEL's" plan to blow up their fleet of heavy equipment to stop the logging operation.

He promptly gets on the phone and calls the ABI to report the aggressive incident.

After he finishes talking to the monotonous agent, he pours some peroxide on the bite wound and puts an antiseptic bandage over it, and angrily says, "I hope they get that little son of a bitch."

Miguel and the Newgen tribe members are driving back to the house, they're all amped up from the adrenaline and Shaun excitingly says to Caleb, "Dude...that was intense, you nailed that lamo in the head, and laid him flat out!" Marco pleasingly adds, "That was so freaking cool, thanks Bro."

They all start sprightly laughing, and playfully slapping Caleb as they continue riding the high from their recent experience.

They're telling Miguel all the juicy details about their stimulating episode as he cautiously navigates his way back to the house.

Back in Afghanistan, the beat up truck transporting the jihadist fighters, pulls up to the terrorist camp in a cloud of hostile dust, and the dedicated fighters enthusiastically jump out and head directly into the main compound to hear Mustafa Rahman, also known as "Rahman the Great," give an inspiring speech to his loyal Islamic Army.

They enter the room that's eerily lit with oil burning lanterns, then carefully lay down their prayer rugs in a ritualistic manner, and humbly kneel on them as their fearless leader majestically walks up to the pulpit.
There's a black backdrop loosely hung up on the wall with the religious symbol of a "star inside a crescent moon" boldly printed on it.

Mustafa proudly looks at his men and charismatically says, "We are the true believers that have been chosen by Allah to continue carrying out his righteous will; this will assure our place in his eternal paradise...We will show *no mercy* to the ones that will not join our blessed holy crusade."

And then he adamantly says, "We must cleanse the world of all infidels and re-establish the state of Islam!"

Everyone in the room immediately stands and starts passionately repeating, "Allahu Akbar." They are completely unaware that an undercover operative from the Monarch of Iran's regime had placed a homing device on the truck when they were in town picking up the fighters, and getting supplies.

Now they NWA have the location of their camp. The Monarch of Iran has been informed by The Ministry of Intelligence. He quickly calls the Air Force General and orders him to immediately scramble the jet fighters with the bunker buster bombs to the known co-ordinance.

The Islamic crusaders are engaging in an appetizing feast called "The Festival of Sacrifice." They're enjoying their favorite dishes like Baida Roti, Chicken Biryani, and Kababs, but little do they know there about to be sacrificed on the altar of genocidal power, and this might be their last supper.

After they finished eating, the Crusaders started playing traditional Islamic music on the djembe and kora as the men festively join in the traditional circle dance.

They suddenly hear the jet fighters approaching and immediately stop the festivities.

Everyone in the room is silent as they confusingly look up at the ceiling awaiting their unknown fate. They hear a paralyzing high pitched whistling, and then the bomb horrendously crashes through the ceiling of the cave-dwelling hitting the floor and mercilessly blowing them all to "Jihadi Paradise."

The Air Force General proudly informs the Monarch about the successful mission.

He is very pleased to hear the Muslim resistance has been eliminated with one fell swoop.

Miguel and the Newgens pull up to the NEL house and quickly go inside eager to tell Jonathan all about the mission.

Jonathan attentively listens as the highly spirited dudes tell him how it all went down, even though it didn't go as planned, he is very proud that they adapted and pulled it off. Jonathan impressively says, "You guys are definitely on your way to becoming proven members of the NEL. All of you displayed Courage on this endeavor, passing one of the nine tests in this mission. Marco, you also displayed faith by noticing, and following the signs of the spirit...Caleb that was an amazing stunt you accomplished. You were willing to risk yourself to save a brother, an example of true sacrifice...Bravo everyone! There's a moment of comradery and Jonathan continues, "You guys are well on your way to achieving the enlightened state of Spiritual Love...I'm not talking about the Worldly love that has been defined as either a superficial physical attraction, kindhearted deeds connected with demoralizing expectations, obsessive desires or perverted pleasure sex...I'm talking about *True Spiritual Love*;

When there's genuine deep care, and concern for one another's well being, physically, mentally, and emotionally. When there's no sexual activity involved.

To prudently guide each other down the path of truth, righteousness, and the sacred way of the wise. Never turning your back on one another, and always standing beside each other, enduring the bad times, and celebrating the good times." Everyone responds in unison "Amen!" There's a comfortable silence, and then Marco innocently asks, "What does it mean when you fall in love?"

Jonathan cheerfully smiles and replies, "That's when a man and women establish a truly spiritual love connection, then exclusively engage in passionate sexual intimacy, and become emotionally linked together as one personality." Marco pleasingly says, "Nice!"

Their spirited assembly comes to a screeching halt when they suddenly hear a special newscast announcement on the television. The broadcaster adamantly says, "This just in;

Russian Dictator Demetri Butinov has miraculously recovered from his gunshot wound to the head, and will be addressing the world tomorrow night at 6pm Central European Time (CET.)

Miguel frighteningly looks at Jonathan and says, "You were right!"

C17

Back in Ireland, Martin Adams of the ERA is completely surprised and devastated as is hears the news about the Dictators recovery. He wonders what went wrong, and starts to feel that maybe God has abandoned him. He suddenly realizes there's going to be serious backlash from the failed attempt.

He disappointingly begins to realize that he and his mates need to keep a low profile and hideout for a little while.

Operations will be much tougher to carry-out now with the NWA on the payback warpath. They will dramatically increase their efforts to locate Martin and shutdown the European resistance. He oddly thinks about his favorite patriarch, ex-IRA leader Michael Collins, and feels like he let his forefather down. He's beginning to lose confidence in the movement.

The Ambassador and governor Grayden are heading down the hostile highway in his well-guarded limousine to the airport, when he gets a call informing him about the attack on the Colorado logging site and the Russian Dictators miraculous recovery.

Ambassador Davidson very impressed says, "Can you believe that? That Ruski is one tough son of a bitch!"

He thinks for a brief moment and realizingly says, "Now that's two NEL incidents in the same area within 5 days of each occurrence, and I have a strong gut feeling they might be based in the general vicinity."

Grayden confidently replies, "That makes sense, we should be able to locate those eco-terrorist bastards quicker with the assistance from the ABI." The Ambassador agreeingly nods.

Now Drake Jackson has been driving for about 8 hours straight, because he thinks the aliens are going to abduct him if he stops driving.

He accidentally looked at one of them when he was getting into his car after leaving work at the drone factory. He is mentally exhausted, extremely tired, and delirious.

He's starting to drive very recklessly, swerving into the other lanes, and his car is running very low on gas. He sees a strange configuration of bright white lights hauntingly approaching, and begins to panic. Drake thinks they're attempting to surround him, so he hastily decides that he would rather die than allow himself to be abducted and violated.

Drake has concluded that he needs to crash his car into the alien spaceship to bring it down, and give the world proof that they really do exist.

After deciding this, he suddenly feels a rapturous sensation of liberation from his schizophrenic fear. A feeling that he hadn't felt in a long time, like when he was a care free teenager, before these complicated emotions made his adult life confusingly difficult.

The intimidating lights are rapidly getting closer, but Drake is not wavering from the dedicated target in his sites, now that he feels like he has found his purpose in life. He is determined to succeed at all costs as he presses down harder on the accelerator, and right before he crashes into them, for a brief moment, he strangely wonders how his life ended here.

Then he loudly yells, "Here's something you can probe, you Pleiadian freaks!" And then there's a thunderous explosion as the two vessels collide.

The Ambassador's limo comes to an unexpected screeching stop. He has just been notified that the lead armored vehicle in his caravan has crashed, head on, into another vehicle.

Drake's car is a mangled pile of twisted metal sprinkled with shattered glass. Car fluids are leaking out like blood from a body. He did not survive the fatal crash, and no longer has to worry about being abducted.

The armored vehicle was damaged and has been immobilized, and the guards had minor injuries.

The emergency vehicles have been dispatched and are on their way to the deadly accident.

The Ambassador fearfully thinks this was an assassination attempt, so the rest of the caravan immediately continues to cautiously escort his limousine to the airport. They safely arrive, and quickly get on the plane that whisks them away to Colorado.

It's another blistering hot day in L.A. as Brian Cheeves wakes up on the floor with his dead wife still in his lap. He has a cold, emotionless look on his face, and feels like an empty shell of a man. He slowly stands up like Lazarus rising from the grave, and then puzzlingly looks around the room as if he doesn't recognize where he's at. After a brief moment of feeling displaced, Brian systematically starts to get ready for work as if he is a programmed robot carrying out his objectives.

He brews up a single K-cup of French roast coffee, and then toasts a plain bagel and evenly spreads some cream cheese on it. He sits at the kitchen table and eats his breakfast like it's just another dreary day. Then as he left to go to work at the broadcast studio, he creepingly says, "Goodbye honey, Have a nice day," and then he casually walks out the door like the horrifying event didn't happen.

He arrives at the studio, and everybody's talking about the miraculous recovery of the Russian Dictator, and are wondering what he might say in his speech tonight.

He sees Steven still working in the control room and feels drawn to him for some unknown reason. Brian walks over by him and curiously stares.

Steven, sensing something odd, looks up and notices Brian starring at him, and starts to get a little paranoid, thinking he might know something about the NEL mission.

The morning news broadcast is about to begin, so Brian stops disturbingly starring at Steven, and begins to carry out his daily duties.

Back at the NEL house, Jonathan and his crew are working out the details to their next mission to go to L.A. and broadcast Jonathan's message of hope. The Newgens have left the house and went back to their regular living situations for the time being, as the crew prepares for the next assignment. Jimmy could only map out a safe route up to Grand Junction, but then he came up with a brilliant idea to white water raft down the Colorado River, to avoid the remaining checkpoints, down to Bullhead City at the point where the California border runs parallel with Arizona, and then cross over.

Miguel adds to the conversation and says," I can arrange for a van to be waiting for us when we cross the border near hwy 40."
Miguel's homeboy Carlos, from his old clique the 18th street gang who is now a gracer, will help them by providing an EV van disguised as a Body Disposal Service vehicle.

It will be equipped with solar panels on the roof to provide a continuous charge, so they can drive the rest of the way without having to stop and recharge to reach their targeted location, and then to escape back to Colorado.

Jimmy with a serious tone says, "I will work on the details of the trip, but I'm guesstimating that it will take around 6 days to raft down the river to the point where we can easily hike down to Bullhead City, and cross over into California. I will find the locations on the river where we can stop along the way, and set up camp for each night. We'll need to leave in two days to get there at the coordinated time."

Jonathan pleasingly responds, "I think this is an excellent idea! Let's work out the details...Okay, it'll be us four going," he gestures to himself, Jimmy, Keshaun, and Miguel. "Ronni, you will stay behind and watch over the safe house, and then meet up with us when we cross back over the border."

Jonathan and his old college buddies use to go on white water rafting trips, so he is well experienced with this type of activity and could easily teach his crew how to maneuver the raft. They're all taking a little break from the brainstorming session to get something to eat. Jimmy is preparing them a meal which consists of egg salad sandwiches and vegetable soup when Miguel intriguingly asks Jonathan, "When Jesus said he was trying to "usher in his kingdom" during the first century, what did he mean?"

Jonathan engagingly answers, "That's an excellent question Miguel. A lot of people have misinterpreted this section of the gospels. Apart from modifying the Torah law; Like forgiving 70 times 7, turning the other cheek, allowing spiritual work on the Sabbath, being married to only one woman, and learning how to properly forgive someone. He was also trying to implement *a true equality* social structure, where everyone is treated equally. Just because you are smarter or stronger than another,

didn't mean you deserved more. You receive the same as the dumb and weak...As long as you're contributing the same amount of effort and utilizing your abilities like everyone else, then you would get the same amount of resources. Everyone gets the necessary items they need to live a comfortable life.
A philosophy professor I once knew told me this story that made a lot of sense."

Then Jonathan tells this story; "There were two men, one is 6'3" and weighs 300lbs, and the other is 5'5" and weighs 150lbs. and they were both hired to carry bricks up a hill. At the end of the day, the larger man was able to carry twice as many bricks as the smaller man. So he asked the man who hired him, "How come I'm getting paid the same amount as the smaller man who only carried half as much as I did?" and the man that hired him answered, "Did you use all your strength and effort to do this job?" And the worker proudly answers, "Yes! The man who hired him then replies, "So did your co-worker...even though he didn't move as many bricks as you did, he used the same amount of effort to move his bricks, so that's why you get the same pay...And that's what it means to be truly equal." Jonathan justly said. Miguel excitingly responds, "Damn! That shit is the real deal! I love it!"

Jonathan continues, "If everyone understood this, we would be one major step closer to a utopian civilization...This is the kind of kingdom Jesus was trying to implement."

Miguel says," What did it mean when Jesus said "Give Caesars what is Caesar's, It has his picture on it, and give God what is God's." Jonathan seriously responds, "Well, the main stream interpretation is that you should give a percentage of your laborious earnings to pay your taxes to the Government, and the rest you keep. But that's not what Jesus meant. The Jews hated paying Roman taxes...What he was actually saying was, Give the Emperor back his manufactured money, corrupt commerce system, unnatural cities, and immoral social structure, And give him back God's natural

Earth and his moralistic way of life, as described in the Mosaic books of the Bible."

Jonathan thinks for a moment and continues, "Jesus was seen by the Romans as a radical revolutionary. He was basically telling the Romans to take everything that they created, and leave God's Earth."

Miguel extremely impressed replies, "Wow...now I understand why the Romans wanted him dead. But why did Caiaphas, the Jewish high priest, want him dead?"

Jonathan sadly answers, "Well, that was part jealousy and pride. Caiaphas took it as a major insult, and claimed it to be an act of heresy. When Jesus claimed he had the authority to modify traditional Jewish laws that they have been practicing and sustaining for over 2500 years...The shock wave it sent down the pious spine of the Jewish community leaders was spiritually devastating. Caiaphas was searingly jealous at the thought that maybe he *was* actually the prophesied messiah."

Miguel extremely impressed with what he just heard says, "That is some heavy shit! He shakes his head in amazement and then says, "What about the people who say Jesus never existed, and it was all just a myth?"
Jonathan excitingly says, "You never cease to amaze me my inquisitive friend...For one thing; There were too many credible witnesses who knew him. And another thing; that's like saying that Julius Caesar, King Herod, Pontius Pilate or the High Priest Joseph Caiaphas didn't exist, I mean you might as well just say the Roman Empire didn't exist, but they did, and so did he!"
Miguel listens with an enlightened look on his face, and nods his head as he comprehends the information that was just relayed to him.

C18

It's now thirty mystifying minutes before the Russian Dictator, Demetri Butinov, gives his inspirational speech. Almost everybody in the world is eagerly waiting to hear about his miraculous experience, like children waiting for Santa Claus to arrive the night before Christmas. Now there seems to be a new admiration starting to grow for their once hated leader, who treacherously enforced unfavorable oppression on them. The ABN will stream a live feed of his speech from the once hallowed grounds of St. Peters Square at the Vatican.

Jonathan and his crew are waiting for the broadcast, and discussing the details of their mission. They've established campsites along the river to stop and rest for the nights.

They will start at Grand Junction, and the first day will make their way to Moab. It will take a couple days to raft down to Page.

Since the dam at Lake Powell has collapsed, they'll be able to continue down towards Lake Mead, and before they get there, they will stop and exit at a strategic point on the river. From there, they can easily hike down to Bullhead City and carefully cross into California.

Jimmy is making a list of the necessary supplies needed to complete their audacious journey.

Ronni will drop them off at Grand Junction, and stay behind to watch over the house, feed the horses and wait for them to return.

Then in the background, like a voice from beyond, they can hear the perplexed announcer on the television saying, "Stay tuned for a special presentation."

Jonathan and his crew stop what they're doing and curiously huddle around the T.V., like voters waiting the outcome of a Presidential election.

The anchorman appears on the screen with a very serious look on his face and says, "Good evening my fellow proselytes; as you may have already heard, three days ago there was a vicious assassination attempt on the Russian Dictators life."

Then with an exuberant tone says, "He miraculously survived the hostile attempt by the ERA, and has lived to talk about it...Now, without further ado, here's the phenomenal Demetri Butinov!" The screen switches to the dictator, who is standing behind a brass colored podium with the NWA emblem on the front of it. But before he speaks, he remembers a very strange dream he had while he was unconscious about a magical serpent, "Gorynych" and now believes he is being protected by the Slavic serpent hero.

He appears to have a luminescent glow of confidence, as he begins to speak in a very calm manner and says; "Hello loyal citizens of the Noble World Alliance;

Earlier this week I was shot in the head by a savage member of the underground, but I have completely recovered," and then assertively says, "I, your invincible Supreme Ruler of the World...LIVES!
I cannot be killed by mere mortal men!"

His voice changes to a more serious tone and says, "We must eliminate this menacing enemy of the people that continues to inflict torment and suffering on us, and our comfortable industrial lifestyle...The NEL are nothing but evil terrorist spreading a message of horror and fear, with the help from their wicked God who wants to destroy us!" He holds up an open hand, and then closes it into a fist and says, "I will crush them all like cockroaches with my mighty army, and end their reign of terror, along with the blasphemous lies they have spoken about their destructive God." Then he reassuringly says, "Stay loyal to the Alliance, and I will protect you from the dangerous vermin plague, that brings hardship and misery." And trying to sound pleasant says,

"Thank you all for support, and enjoy the rest of your evening."

The screen switches back to the anchorman and he vivaciously says, "That was an extremely inspiring, and exceptionally well spoken speech!

He hesitates for a brief moment and says, "This ends our special presentation."

Jonathan and his crew are completely dumbfounded about what they have just heard. They're looking at each other with utter amazement.

Jonathan disappointingly says, "Just another spin doctor, twisting the truth and prolonging the Grand Illusion"

Miguel enthusiastically says, "But you called it Jonah...and then it happened!"

"As it is written, so shall it be!" Jonathan casually replied.

Then he calmly walks out the back door into the welcoming woods, to a solitary place where he goes to meditate, his holy sanctuary.

After a brisk quarter mile walk through the dense forest, he arrives at a secluded cave, walks in, and lights four candles representing the four corners of the Earth.

Then he lays down on a handmade Persian rug, that's in the middle of the room, and falls into a relaxed state of consciousness and completely disconnects from all the events occurring in his life. And then in the calm silence, he mentally starts speaking to the inner voice of the spirit and solemnly says, "Is there any way that we can stop the next phase of tribulations from occurring?"

And the inner voice answers, "Anything is possible with the lord. That's why we're giving you a chance, by delivering the "Message of Liberation."If you can get through to the people on Earth, then there will be hope for the future."

Jonathan hopefully responds, "Then I shall do my best to get through to them."

He comes out of his meditative state with a strong feeling of great hope. As he's walking back to the house, he starts to think that maybe the NEL could finish ushering in the heavenly kingdom here on Earth, without any more devastating plagues, or deadly conflicts happening.

Back at the White House the exclusive red phone enigmatically rings as Monarch Ronald Spade walks over as if he's dreading the call, and slowly answers.

It's Demetri Butinov on the other end, and he says, "Hello comrade, have you found out who is leading this irritating resistance?"

Monarch Spade responds, "Nothing yet sir, but we have a very promising lead."

Butinov intimidatingly continues, "Must I remind you of all the assistance I gave your political career before the collapse happened. And after the collapse, I appointed you to the position you currently hold...So, now it's time for you to return the favor."

And then angrily says, "I want you to find their leader, and bring him to me! We know he's operating out of your territory."

Monarch Spade fearfully says, "Yes sir, I'll do my best."

"Don't disappoint me or they're will be serious consequences!" And then Demetri hangs up.

Ambassador Davidson and Governor Grayden have just arrived in Colorado, and are meeting with the ABI agent, Scott Aldrich, at the logging site. He's in charge of investigating the logging site attack, and the Conversion Center escape.

The short, stocky, slightly overweight Caucasian man, walks up to them and introduces himself and then says, "I have already talked to everyone involved, and they all said the same thing, that a bunch of teenagers attempted to sabotage the heavy equipment... They used a diversionary tactic to distract everyone and put sugar water in the tanks, which would have damaged the engines...But what's puzzling is the fact that they blew up one of the dozers with dynamite."

Davidson inquisitively asks, "Did the loggers provide a description of the teenagers?" Aldrich firmly replies, "Yes, they said they were well-bred white boys, except for one, who was a Native American...I'm heading over to the Conversion Center, so I can examine where the escape took place."

Davidison replies, "Okay, we'll go with you"

The three of them get into the Ambassadors limousine, and speedily drive away to the center.

Capt. Willard is in his office, finishing the tedious report about the humiliating escape. He is not looking forward to meeting with the ABI agent. Sgt. Pervace softly knocks on the door, and the Captain tells him to enter.

Pervace alarmingly says, "There here!"

Willard slowly rises from his bureaucratic desk to go out and greet the distressing agent. As he's walking down the hallway, he can see them anxiously waiting in the lobby and thinks, "this is probably not going to go well."

As he reluctantly enters the lobby, he immediately walks over to the Ambassador and respectfully says, "It's nice to see you again sir." They shake hands, and the Ambassador says, "This is Agent Aldrich of the ABI. Willard shakes his hand and says, "I'm very grateful for your assistance with this extremely embarrassing matter."

Aldrich slightly annoyed replies, "The Monarch has a major "hard on" for this one, especially after the attempt on the Dictators life... So what do you have for us?"
Willard, in a very professional manner says, "Well, basically the detainee over took the guard, took the keys, and then ran out the front door to fellow members of the NEL, who were waiting just past the tree line. I have a copy of the complete report for everyone." He passes them out, and they begin reading through it. Agent Aldrich says, "I see here it states that they used dynamite on the fence and guard station."
Willard responds, "Yes, that is correct"

Aldrich continues, "It also states that they rode away on horseback."

Willard adds, "That's right."

Aldrich, "Did they check to see which direction the horse tracks were heading?"

Willard nervously replies, "I'm afraid to say, no. But I wanted to let you know that we did get a detailed description of the horseback rider who threw the dynamite."

The agent reacts to his response with mild indifference. He reads the report a little more, and realizes the connection of the dynamite being used at both crime scenes.

Agent Aldrich says, "I want to examine the areas involved with the escape."

Willard answers, "Certainly." And then asks, "Have you received any legitimate tips after releasing the photo?"

Aldrich quickly responds, "We're still thoroughly checking into the information we have received, but nothing yet."

And then sternly says, "We'll let you know as soon as we get something substantial."

Willard is sensing the agent's displeasure as he leads them out to examine the critical areas where the shameful escape took place.

C19

Back at the broadcast center, Steven has just finished upgrading the networking system with new interface software. But it also included a program that will allow him to override all broadcasts to transmit Jonathan's speech everywhere.

He's starting to get really scared after hearing the dictator's speech, because he thinks that they're probably going to increase security at the facility, and Jonathan might have a difficult time getting through the gate. He grabs his pack, and cautiously walks over to Brian and says, "I've completed the software upgrade."

Brian uninterestingly nods. Steven suspiciously continues, "You'll need to reboot the system before you close down the set, so it's ready for tomorrows broadcast."

Brian hesitates for an awkward moment, and then unexpectedly comes out and painfully says, "Did you know that my wife poisoned our children, and then herself, to death, just yesterday?"

Steven shocked about what he just heard, stumblingly replies, "Oh, really?"
Brian awkwardly continues, "She believed she was cursed, because she accepted the Bio Chip, and rejected her beloved God."
There's a brief silence, and then Brian breaks down and starts grievously crying.

Steven uncomfortably rubs his back trying to console him. And then Brian desperately asks, "Do you think God will forgive her?" Steven has a moment of uncertainty, and doesn't know what to say to him. After that uncomfortable moment passes Brian says, "Thank you for your compassion." He confusingly looks around, and then awkwardly gets up and walks away.

Back at NEL house, the crew is just about finished packing all the needed supplies for their dangerous journey to California.

Jimmy checked the raft to make sure there weren't any leaks in it, and is now sharpening everyone's Ka-Bar fighting knife. Jimmy taught the crew members hand to hand combat using the lethal knife, and now they all carry one for self defense purposes.

Jonathan is feeling a stronger sense of urgency, that it's even more important now than ever, to deliver his hopeful liberating message to the people in the world because of the Dictators damning speech. They need to leave early in the morning if they're going to make to the broadcast center in time to meet up with Steven.

Ronni is feeling restless, so she's decided to go out jogging to burn off some of her anxious energy. She briskly runs down the pitted dirt road that leads from the house to the highway, and when she gets to the end of the mile long road, she notices her shoelace is untied, and casually bends down to tie it.

Then looks up and notices a car has pulled over to the side of the road, and is changing out a flat tire.

She starts to feel a little suspicious. The person now seems to be looking, and pointing at her. She suddenly remembers her face is being broadcasted around the area as a dangerous fugitive, and quickly turns and starts frantically running back to the house.

Jonathan and Keshaun are engaged in an intense discussion about biblical prophecies in the kitchen, and Jonathan disappointingly says, "Do you know what the most frustrating thing about understanding the prophecies in Revelations, and knowing the terrifying things that are going to happen to mankind in the near future is?"

Keshaun trying to be funny replies, "Ummm... That you would get bored with life because, you already know the outcome?"

Jonathan slightly amused says, "No..."then sadly says, "It's the fact that you cannot change the course of disastrous events, no matter what you do."

Keshaun agreeing replies, "Yeah, that's one heavy boulder to drag around." Miguel casually walks in and says, "It's all set up; he'll have the van ready and waiting for us."

Jonathan, in his sadness, pleasingly nods.

Then Ronni unexpectedly crashes through the front door, startling everyone, almost out of breath and says, "I think I might have been spotted."

Jonathan, "What do you mean?"

Ronni, catching her breath says, "I mean, I ran down to the end of the dirt road where it connects with the highway, and I saw someone changing a flat tire, and we made eye contact. I can tell by their reaction that they might have recognized me."

Jonathan, trying to keep his cool concerningly says, "Okay, are you alright? Did you put up the camouflage barrier to cover the entrance?" Ronni replies, "Oh shit! I forgot!"

There's a chain-link gate that has living bushes attached on it, to hide the road leading to the safe house.

Jonathan calmly says, "Okay...Keshaun? Can you take care of that?"

Keshaun responds, "No problem coach. I'm on it." He bolts out the door, like it's the critical game-winning play.

Jonathan firmly tells Ronni, "You need to start wearing a disguise when you go out." She agreeingly nods.

Back at the conversion center, Ambassador Davidson decides to set up a massive search operation to find Ronni, and focus all his resources in the Boulder City area. Based on the local Eco-terrorist activities, and the sightings reported, that seems to be the central point.

He plans to saturate the area with Enforcer Squads and drone patrols, using the latest face, voice, and body recognition equipment.

There's no need for search warrants anymore, if they suspect anything, they're allowed to search any premises they choose.

And if it isn't bad enough already that the citizens feel their souls have been diabolically violated because they were forced to pledge allegiance to NWA, but now they're also reminded that their civil liberties no longer exist. They will begin their unsavory sweep, in a ten-mile radius of the area, at first dawn.

C20

It's another unpleasantly warm December
evening, as the western part of the oppressed
world sombrely sleeps. The horrifyingly new
day is getting ready to unpleasantly greet them,
just beyond the fiery horizon.

Jonathan unnervingly wakes up from another
emotionally intense dream. It's was about a
barbarous army of two-legged pelican spiders,
that were mercilessly coming after him and the
others. He feverishly jumps out of bed, already
knowing what the dream means, and rapidly
wakes up everyone in the house and anxiously
says, "We have been compromised! We need
to leave immediately, or were not going to be
able to make it out of the area in time."

Everybody confusingly gets out of bed and
Keshaun says, "What's going on?"

Jonathan answers, "They're going to aggressively net sweep this area today."
Keshaun puzzlingly asks, "How do you know that?
"I had a dream last night," replied Jonathan.
Miguel shockingly says, "You mean another spirit message?"
Jonathan solemnly answers, "Yes, Miguel, a spiritual message from God's hotline."
"Okay, say no more," replied Miguel.
They all hectically scramble to get their packs organized. The truck is already loaded with all the heavy gear.

Jimmy disguised the truck to look like it is part of the NWA military fleet, so they will easily blend in, and hopefully won't draw any unnecessary attention.
Jonathan says, "Okay gang let's take a moment to say a prayer and share a meal before we set sail." Everyone comes into the living room and he kneels down on one knee, and then says,

"Lord, when your kingdom come, then *all* of our will, will be down." There's a brief silence, then everyone says there, "Amen."

They all enjoy a delicious triple berry smoothie and a peanut butter protein bar before they head out the door to the next phase of their unearthly adventure.

As they're driving down the combative highway, Ronni slips a disk into the car stereo, and the Guns and Roses song "Paradise City" starts to play.

They all start singing along to the chorus, "Take me down to The Paradise City where the grass is green and the girls are pretty, Take! Me! Home!"

Right after they get to the outskirts of Boulder City, an unfriendly swarm of helicopters and drones, like a fast moving storm cloud of demonized locust, intimidatingly buzz into the area. A caravan of transport vehicles aggressively moves in right behind the overwhelming swarm.

Squads of enforcers threateningly march around the frightened city, like the ruthless Schutzstaffel searching for Jews in Germany during World War II, trying to locate the hostile agitators. "Woe to the inhabitants of the earth who will live in these treacherous times."

They're conducting thorough house to house searches, using four soldier units, who are violently interrupting people lives in pursuit of the NEL terrorists. The house they're currently getting ready to brutally violate is right next door to Takoda's house. He silently watches as the Enforcers mercilessly blast their way into the neighbor's house, and begin interrogating them.

He's getting very concerned, and believes they're looking for him, but they're actually looking for Ronni. He can hear their agonizing screams and starts to get scared. He climbs up to the musty attic and hides in a large cardboard box filled with old smelly blankets.

Soon they will be at his house. He knows that his adoptive parents will be barbarously interrogated, and their sentimentally valued possessions are going to be smashed to pieces. He can foresee the anguish they will soon experience, and knows the horrifying pain they will soon be feeling, because of the deep emotional bond he shares with them.

While he's hiding, he thinks back when he used to spend time with his great grandfather, "Singing Hawk," and all the stories he used to tell him about their ancestors. One of his favorite stories is about Geronimo.

The great warrior, who once was a peaceful tribesman, fell madly in love with the most beautiful women in the tribe. She became his wife, and they had two adorable children together. They were living a simple life in harmony with nature, and maintaining a peaceful balance with the neighboring tribes.

And then his family was brutally murdered by government soldiers trying to eradicate his people, while he was on a trading mission, and that's what set him off on his historical campaign of deadly retribution. The same instinctual impulse to want to protect his guardians burns deep inside him, almost compelling him to jump back down, like a super hero, and defend them. But he knows that would not be a wise idea, because he would be no match standing up against four armed enforcers. So he stays strong, and does not give into that primal impulse, and keeps quietly still.

The search squad is now at their front door, and instead of knocking, they vigorously kick the door down and rush inside to find the elderly couple sitting on the couch in utter fear. The squad leader intimidatingly walks up to them and shows the picture of Ronni and disrespectfully asks, "Have any of you old bags seen this woman?"

Takoda's guardian corporately replies, "No sir, I've never seen this woman before in my life." One of the enforcers notices the slightly hidden door that leads to the attic and waves his partner over to assist.

His guardian, who has been like a mother to him, runs towards the soldiers and falls to her knees and begs them to stop. The enforcer brutally kicks her. She falls back and hits her head and passes out. He quickly points his rifle at her husband and says, "Stay back, old man, or I'll smack you dead with lead...Bring me a ladder, quick!"

Takoda, still hiding in the box, is starting to feel like a coward, and begins to rethink the situation. He comes to the conclusion that he needs to make a run for it, because he knows he's out gunned, and any aggressive reaction would be suicide. Then he thinks back on what he learned about, "keeping your cool, when the situation gets hot," so don't make any hastily foolish decisions.

The attic door slams open, BAM!! Then Takoda immediately reaches for an aluminum bat in a box full of baseball gear, and quickly runs up to the attic opening. As the enforcer pops his head up, Takoda catches him off guard and repeatedly bashes him in the head until his helmet flies off, and he falls like a bag of bricks, to the unforgiving floor.

The enforcers below begin spraying the ceiling full of lead brimstone, as he quickly makes his way over to the attic window.
He smashes the glass and runs onto the roof, then jumps off and races into the dense wilderness.
The angry enforcers scramble out of the house after him, but he has vanished like the "spirit in the wind."

The squad leader reports the hostile encounter to his commander, and then the commander immediately relays the incident to Ambassador Davidson.
The Ambassador is morose because Takoda got away, but he's even more upset that he has to spend his precious time hunting down these irritating parasites, instead of enjoying his worldly life. He strongly believes that it's all about getting everything you can from this world while you're alive because when you die, that's it, your life is over.

He remembers the conversation he had with agent Aldrich about the native Indian at the logging terrorist attack, and quickly contacts the agent to inform him about the recent development. Aldrich hurriedly heads over to Takoda's guardians house, to follow up on the incident, and to further interrogate the already terrified elderly couple.

Jonathan and his crusading crew are half way to Grand Junction, when Ronni out of the blue says, "Do you know why so many people like to do drugs, like heroin and cocaine?" Jonathan thinks back to the time when he went through his experimental drug phase in college, and obligingly replies, "No, why do they like them so much?"

She spiritly responds, "Because living in the industrial world sucks!" she laughs, "And because we loved that blissful, euphoric sensation you get anytime you do them. We were chasing that heavenly feeling!" And then she suddenly realizes something else and says,

"And they come from plants which God created…maybe it's a way to keep people deeply connected to the natural Earth, rather than the material world." Jonathan a little surprised with her comment responds,
"That's a very unusual theory; I know people use manufactured and natural drugs to ease emotional and physical pain. But remember; when you get your new spiritual body, you will no longer feel any more pain.

   And another thing; when you reach a higher level of understanding God, and are truly filled with the Holy Spirit, then you won't need those types of drugs to make you feel euphoric anymore.

Ronni understandingly says, "Amen! The way of the wise, maintaining a balanced and righteous lifestyle."

Jonathan flashes the NEL hand sign, and she flashes it back.

Then Ronni slips a disc into the stereo and cranks up the music. It's a D-Kool Cat song called "Spiritually High." And as it starts playing, she soulfully sings along.

The other members are amusingly entertained, and begin laughing as they watch Ronni rock out. Jimmy continues driving the spirited crew to the drop off point.

Brian is waking up to another morbidly bizarre morning as he continues to grieve for his family for the fourth straight day. Even though the smell of rotting flesh is starting to become unbearable, he can't find the strength to let them go, and allow the CDS (corpse disposal service) to pick-up the bodies.

His sorrow is turning into deep disdainful anger that is now directed towards the new world order. He blames them for the tragic events that happened to his beloved family.

He's sitting on the couch, staring into the empty abyss of his life, and then begins dementedly mumbling to himself, "I think I can save her from Dante's inferno."

Brian starts to believe that if he dies a noble death, he will be able to plead for his wife's sin to be absolved, and then they can be reunited with their children in heaven.

He reluctantly gets ready for work, eats a piece of burnt toast, and then hesitantly walks out the door to continue his painfully dreadful existence. But now has a very small glimmer of hope in his grim situation.

Jonathan and his rebellious crew have safely made it to the Grand Junction launching site, and are slowly pulling into the almost deserted campground. As they drive in, they cautiously check around the area for any possible hostile threats. All they can see is a couple of harmless looking tents at some of the camp sites. Jimmy parks the truck, and the gang climbs out and starts unloading the gear. Keshaun starts thinking about what Jonathan said after the Dictators speech, about the Grand Illusion, and curiously asks, "What did you mean when you said, the dictator is prolonging the Grand Illusion?"

Jonathan gladly replies, "Well, that's the concept about the petroleum industrial world, being portrayed as the way life's supposed to be, when in fact it's not...We should be living in an Eden style paradise. A world where a variety of beautiful flowers growing freely, emitting their pleasant aromas as the wind blows the blissfully scented air, pleasing your sense of smell. And you ride an Arabian horse through luscious green pastures, filled with various trees and colorful plants that grow freely, that can be seen for miles. Groves of nourishing fruit and vegetable trees grow on low level valleys and hillsides, alongside ground growing crops, as the rain drops it's miraculous waters at exactly the precise times to keep everything healthy. A place where there's a variety of talented birds singing their melodic songs, and displaying fascinating air spectacles all day long. The other small creatures and insects do their job eating the excess of fallen fruits and vegetables, like servants cleaning up after a fabulous feast..."

"All the amazing land and sea mammals are extremely playful and friendly, and are provided for our amusement..."

"This is the magical Earth we should be living in, not the unnatural industrial world that's destroying it."

Everyone stopped what they were doing and were hypnotically fixed on the imagery Jonathan was describing.

Then he pleasantly says, "This is my dream... Let's set up camp and prepare for a celebratory feast tonight before we get some sleep. We need to leave at first dawn."

Jonathan inflates the six-man Alibaba raft, Keshaun and Miguel set up the Ozark tents, and Ronni collects some dead wood and starts a blazing hot fire in the bonfire pit, as Jimmy prepares the festive meal of fresh trout, that he caught fresh out of the river, balsamic rice, and power greens salad for his fellow crew members.

Everybody continues to complete their necessary tasks, as the sun is pleasantly setting behind the monumental mountains.

Jimmy has finished preparing the dinner, and calls them over.

They all sit around the warm, comforting, fire, and listen to the crackling flames mixed together with the soothing sounds of the rushing river waters in the background, and Jonathan gets everyone's attention and says, "I would like to say a little prayer," everyone goes quiet.

"Thanks, Lord, for watching over us, and guiding us, through this very bizarre journey. Amen" There's a brief moment of silence, and then he enthusiastically says, "Let's begin the feast!"

They pleasantly partake in a delicious meal and share in some jovial fellowship under the translucent night sky, that's beautifully filled with stars that sparkle like moonlit diamonds.

They can still take a moment to appreciate the beauty of God's creation, amidst the animosity in the treacherous time they're living in. And even amongst all these adversities, they're still able to hold on to their sacred beliefs.

C21

It's another dreadful day as the enforcers continue their fatal sweep of the Boulder City area. Ambassador Davidson is very disappointed that the search squad wasn't able to apprehend Takoda and interrogate him. The name of the NEL leader still eludes him. He's dreading the phone call he will soon have to make to the Monarch, to update him about the unfortunate event.

Takoda has made his way over to the NEL safe house, just to find out that no one's there. The drones are curiously buzzing around above, looking for Ronni and their new added objective, to also locate Takoda. He needs to take cover, so he decides to break into the house. He tries to break a window with his elbow, but it doesn't break, because it's made of polycarbonate, or also known as bulletproof glass. Next he tries to pick the security lock on the solid oak wood door. It takes him about an hour, but he's able to gain access inside the house. He walks inside and looks around, and then notices that the lights are on in the kitchen and suspiciously says, "Is there anyone here?" No one answers.

He goes into the kitchen just to double check, and confirms that no ones in there.
The kitchen is empty, so while he's in there, he decides to make himself something to eat. He's eating some hard boiled eggs and vegetables, and curiously looks through the house for any interesting objects or memorabilia, and stumbles onto Jonathan's journal. As he reads through it, he comes to a page that's describing an encounter that his friend Jeremiah had, with some kind of spacecraft, when he was in the Pacific Northwest that descended down from the sky in a cloud of smoke and fire. Very similar to the experience Moses had. Jeremiah was also transported up into the vessel.

Once inside the craft, he gazed upon a pellucid humanoid being that shone like the sun, and spoke without moving his lips, and said with a thunderous voice, "Go and warn the people of Earth of the coming plagues."

Back at the campsite Jimmy has just awakened from an unsettling nightmare about the mutilated boy from Iraq and chillingly screams. Jonathan rushes over to his tent and concerningly asks, "Are you alright?" Jimmy unnervingly replies, "The little boy's ghost from Iraq is haunting my dreams." "There are no ghost's Jimmy. Everyone's soul goes to the land of dead when you die to rest until Resurrection Day." Jonathan calmly replied. Jimmy asks, "Then why do I have these nightmares?"

"Those are demons preying on your guilt and fears, trying to mess with your head to throw you off track. Stay strong and pray, and they will cease." Jonathan comfortingly answered. Jimmy feeling relieved says, "Okay...Thanks."

Jonathan's crew start breaking down the tents, packing up the gear and putting it in the raft, when Jonathan concerningly says to Ronni, "You should stay here a couple nights until things cool off in the city." She agreeingly nods.

The crew members put on their safety vests, and are now ready to enter the formidable river. He gives a last-minute pep talk and says, "Make sure to pay attention to my commands, because I'll be reading the river for the safest route to take, and it's critical that we row in unison to make sure we stay in control of the raft." Jimmy replies, "Aye Aye, Captain."

They drag the raft over to the river side and push it in. They all climbed aboard, grab their paddles, and sit in their strategically assigned seats.

Jonathan gives them the hand signal to go, and they start rowing down the rhythmic river. Ronni watches her friends fade away into the distance as the river slowly moves them into an uncertain future.

The crew is having a blast, like kids in an amusement park, riding the white water rafting ride in adventure land.

They've been at it all day, rolling up and down the melodic waves, and dangerously swerving from side to side, as the water indiscriminately splashes over each them. They're starting to get tired, just as they arrive at their designated campsite in Moab.

They paddle to shore, get out of the raft and set up camp for the night.

The next morning they awaken to the unpleasant sound of a gang of eight obnoxious skin-heads, some of them carry bats, making their way down to the river-side, screaming and yelling profanities at each other in a playful manner.

Jonathan and his crew immediately get dressed, grab their fighting knives, and stand in a relaxed V-shaped fighting formation. The skin head leader walks up to them, and with a very creepy tone says, "What do we have here? A wetback, a nigger, a kike, and a traitor!

I think it's time to teach these queers a lesson in ethnicity cleansing."

The rest of his gang starts laughing and getting fired up for an old school style beat down. Jonathan calmly replies, "you really shouldn't discriminate by race...Only by religious deity and moralistic doctrine, or in your case, lack of." The skin head gang leader looks slightly puzzled and says, "Are you trying to confuse me with your religious bullshit?"

Jonathan casually says, "I'm just trying to enlighten you."

Skin head replies, "Fuck your enlightenment!" Jonathan and his crew flash their Ka-Bar fighting knives, like the old world Jewish zealots, "The Sicarii."

These were the hardcore Jewish fighters that went up against the mighty Roman soldiers during the last revolt in the first century A.D.

Jonathan looks the leader in the eyes and intimidatingly shouts out a screeching yell, like the native Indian battle cry,

"WOOO YAYAYAYA WOOO!" When they heard that, the skin head gang suddenly became paralyzed with fear.
Jonathan and his crew watched their faces, as every ounce of misguided courage was completely draining out of them. They all turned and ran as fast as they could back into the woods, like scared little rabbits.

   After the last cowardly skin head faded away into the dark density, they all start mildly laughing, and Jonathan says, "A little bit of Spirit Magic!"And then informedly says, "Just separating the Wheat from the Chaff."
Keshaun asks, "What does that mean?"

   Jonathan answers," Well, there are people who understand the way of the wise, and there are people who don't. And you need to learn to separate them." Keshaun nods. They pack up the gear, and continue rolling down the river.

   Brian Cheeves is starting his shift at the broadcast studio, and after doing his daily duties, he goes to the AV tech department looking for Steven Ferris. He's a little concerned that Steven might have informed his superiors about what he told him, "that his wife killed herself, and his children." Because then they'll send the CDS to take the bodies away before he's able to complete his noble deed.

Steven sees Brian entering the department and starts to get a little paranoid, so he quickly ducks out another exit. Steven thinks that Brian might know something about his plan to clear out the broadcast center, and sneak Jonathan into the studio to broadcast his speech. He's feeling a panic attack coming on. It starts with intense discomfort, followed with accelerated heart rate and profuse sweating. He rushes to the bathroom to splash some water on his face, and then locks himself inside a stall to ride out the attack.

Brian anxiously asks the supervisor, "It's very important that I talk to Steven about the system upgrades he applied. Is he here?"

The Supervisor replies, "Yeah, he should be at his workstation, let me go get him." He walks over there but does not see him, and comes back and says, "He's not over there; he must be in one of the studios."

Brian nervously says, "Okay, thanks," and then hastily leaves the department.

Agent Aldrich has just arrived at Takoda's guardian house, and is getting ready to question the elderly man, and with a creepingly calm tone asks," What's your name?"

He hesitantly answers, "William Getz."

"Okay, Bill, how long has Takoda been living here?" Aldrich inquisitively asked.

He doesn't like being called Bill because that was his American nickname, and he passionately hates them, because after the collapse happened, the Americans betrayed the Jews. "Please don't call me Bill. Either call me Will, or William," He solemnly replied.

The agent looks him in the eye, and gives him a "How dare you tell me what to do" expression. Then firmly slaps him in the face and sternly says, "I'm not fond of playing games, *Bill*...you either answer my questions or I'm going to have your wife shot.

William can see that he is deadly serious. He can't bear the thought of seeing his wife's brains being blown on the wall, and becoming some madman's morbid work of sick art, so he breaks down and shamefully says, "Right after the collapse happened; we were paid to hide him."

"By Whom?" Aldrich firmly asked.

"A lawyer representing a very famous couple," William quickly replied. Aldrich continues to aggressively interrogate him and asks, "Who does he usually hang out with?"

"I don't really know...these other kids from the area. He's a quiet and reserved young man, and doesn't really tell us much." William vaguely replied.

"I see." Aldrich unexpectedly pulls out his gun, points it at his wife's head, and coldly shoots. She immediately falls to the ground, convulsing, as the blood runs out of her head like a can of spilled red paint.

William runs to her side, trying not to cry and grievously calls out her name, "Julia!"

Aldrich says, "Now that I got your complete attention...who does he maliciously cohort with?

William is extremely distraught, and with every ounce of courage he has left, he looks up at him and says, "Go to hell you heartless Nazi bastard."

Aldrich shaking his head sarcastically says, "No...that would be very rude. I insist that you go first." In one fluid motion, he points and fires the gun. It happened so quickly, that Will died with a surprised look frozen on his face.

After a brief silence, Aldrich nonchalantly says to the enforcers, "He couldn't have gotten too far, keep searching the area."

Jonathan and his crew made it to Page safely, and camped there without incident. They continued onward to the exit point of the river, got out, and are now setting up camp for the night. They need to be well rested so they have enough energy to hike down to the vehicle that's waiting for them across the California border.

Jonathan sees a flickering light in the distance that reminds him of the comforts of a loving grandparent, and decides to check it out. There's a cabin on the lower side of the hill. He has an overwhelming feeling of curiosity, so he walks up to the diminutive dwelling and lightly knocks on the door.

A prominent elderly Caucasian women, dressed like a Navajo Indian chieftess answers and says, "I have been expecting you Jonathan. It brings me great joy to see you, please come in and have a seat, let me get you something refreshing to drink."

She goes into the kitchen and get's a couple of glasses of lemonade. Jonathan, feeling like a kid again, sits down. She comes back and hands him a glass, and politely says, "Excuse my manners. My name is Madeline." and then casually says, "I know of your mission that the Great Spirit has sent you on..."The Blue Star" must make his appearance in order to usher in the Fifth World...I was informed in a dream that

I will bear witness to his unveiling." This is a well known Hopi Indian prophecy.

They momentarily experience a déjà vu sensation. Jonathan drinks his lemonade while he amusingly smiles at her.

And then she says, "I have prepared a delicious meal for you and your friends. Baked Pheasant, with a mixed berry glaze, wild rice, and butter squash for you and your tribe to enjoy."

She gives him the prepared foods and excitingly says, "I also have a gift for you" she hands him a necklace with a turquoise bear that symbolizes courage, strength, and leadership.

He gratefully takes the generous offerings, thanks her and gives her a long affectionate hug, and then enchantingly walks back to the campsite to rejoin his crew. Jimmy concerningly asks, "Where have you been?" He replies, "I just took a walk to the cabin up there." He points to the hillside, but the light is no longer shining, it's almost like the cabins no longer there.

What do you mean? Jimmy puzzlingly asked.
Jonathan also a little puzzled says, "Never mind;
an Angel made us a meal, so let us partake until
we are full, and then get some sleep. We have a
very busy day tomorrow."
After finishing their feast, they bed down for
the night. Jonathan is having a vivid dream that
was about being euphorically raptured up into
the sky. He feels a sensation of complete
release from all negative emotions. Like a
heavy, burdensome load of depressing baggage
has been lifted, as he's gently lifted up through
the comforting clouds.
 Then he's awoken just before dawn by a black
crow cawing. He quickly wakes the rest of the
crew. They slowly crawl out of their tents, and
begin getting ready for their hike down to the
border, and Jonathan says, "Just bring what you
need and leave the rest behind."
Jimmy is done packing, and he's looking at the
map, studying the dangerous path they will
soon travel.

Miguel inquisitively asks Jonathan, "When your friend Jeremiah was warning everybody about the coming plagues and then just disappeared. How come you didn't go with him?" Jonathan, remembering the deep, painful, regret he felt when that happened, simply says, "Because I didn't believe him."

Miguel understandingly nods. After eating a quick breakfast of natural power bars, nuts, and dried fruit, they all grab their back-packs and start walking down the mountainous trail. Halfway down the beaten path, they come upon a crudely assembled tent city, and the people are oddly gathered around a bar-b-que pit, like demons performing a ritualistic sacrifice.

The crew stops and curiously observes the unusual activity for a few minutes unnoticed. Then one of the dwellers notices them, and slurringly screams, "Flesh meat!"
The group turns to look at Jonathan and his crew. The crew pulls out there knives and get ready for a possible fatal confrontation.

The leader of this peculiar group of patrons walks fearlessly up to Jonathan.

He has a wicked look in his eyes, and his body is slightly shaking and trembling. Then with slurred speech says, "Would you like to join us for a bite to eat?" Jonathan suddenly realizes their cannibals.

The leader then mysteriously changes his tone, and now has a steady voice, says,

"Well if it isn't Jonathan, the loyal crusader of God." Jonathan is surprised that he knows his name, and realizes he's now talking to the Demon that has possessed the body.

He replies with an authoritative tone,

"Demon, I command you with authority granted to me by the Son, to leave this man's body."

The demon dementedly laughs and says, "Nice try Jonathan, but this is our time, and you have no power over me."

And then, without hesitation, Jonathan slashes the leader's throat. The other dwellers stand there in shock, not knowing what to do.

Jonathan looks down at the dead leader and says, "You're wrong, demon!"

The other crew members follow suit as they begin methodically slaughtering some of the demon flesh eaters.

After they kill a couple of them, the rest turn and run frantically into the woods. Joshua and his crew quickly leave the area and continue hiking down the trail to make sure they get to the border on time.

Keshaun looks back and can see some of the dwellers gathering up there dead to probably eat them.

The mystical sun is slowly setting as they make it to the border crossing and meet up with Miguel's homeboy, Carlos.

Miguel gives him a brotherly hug and makes quick introductions. They hurriedly get into the back of the CDS van and start driving down the interstate to their targeted destination, L.A.

C22

It's the crucial day for the mission as Steven Ferris nervously gets ready for work. He decided to call in sick for the last two days, because he's trying to avoid Brian. He has been in an emotional wrestling match with his mortal fear, and is still having waves of doubt about participating in this dangerous operation. Another panic attack is starting to overtake him when he suddenly shouts out, "Lord, please give me the strength!"

Then instantly he has a calming sensation rush through his timid body. His anxiety and fear quickly fade, like a super hero who is transforming into their powerful alter ego. He continues getting dressed, and then enthusiastically whisks out the door to the adventurous day awaiting him.

He arrives at the studio and reports to the tech department. He gets the "burner phone" that his going to use to call in the bomb threat, out of his desk and puts it in his pocket. He's focused and feeling extremely confident that everything will go as planned.

Brian has just arrived at the studio and is still worried about Steven. He hasn't seen him in the studio for a couple days.

He goes to the tech department and peeks his head in the door, he sees Steven sitting at his station.

He's relieved and decides not to engage with him. Instead, he's going to periodically follow him around today, but for the time being, he's going to go back to complete his daily duties.

Jonathan and his crew are holding up at Carlos's house, which is about an hour's walk away from the studio.

Jonathan tells the guys, "I'm going to walk to the studio, instead of driving." He thinks it will be easier to lose someone on foot, if he runs into any problems.

Miguel immediately says, "I'm gonna go with you, as back up, because, this me Barrio!" Jonathan agrees, because they will blend in a lot easier, and Miguel knows the area.

It's now 1:30; Ambassador Davidson and agent Aldrich are fiercely closing in on the NEL house. Ronni and Takoda apprehensively hide out in the basement, because it's well insulated and it will cover their heat signature.

At the studio, Brian is stealthily following Steven as he's getting ready to phone in the bomb threat, but for a brief moment, Steven is thinking about betraying Jonathan and becoming a hero for the NWA.

Jonathan and Miguel are cautiously heading down to the broadcast center, making their way through the crowded city streets of depressed people, and are now standing across the street from the entrance.
Jonathan quietly says, "Okay Miguel, wait for me at that Italian restaurant across the street." Miguel, feeling a little concerned replies, "Si mon...Live strong and Die free"

Jonathan flashes him the NEL hand sign and walks over to the entrance. He stops for a moment and sees a spider crawling up a light pole, and hopes this isn't a trap.
He hesitantly walks over to the guard station and flashes the fake ID badge to the guard... The guard pauses, then waves him through. Then he goes to the side door and enters the access code, he quietly opens the door and carefully walks in. He quickly makes his way to the mainframe room next to the studio, uses the copied key to unlock the door, and is now hiding out there.

Steven walks into the restroom with Brian shadowing him, but Brian doesn't enter. He waits outside. Steven hesitates for a moment...and then calls in the diversionary bomb threat.

The security sirens loudly blare out there warning song and a commanding voice comes over the intercom and says, "Please go to the nearest exit, and evacuate the building immediately!"

It's extremely chaotic as everybody frantically rushes towards the exits. Steven makes his way up to the main studio, but to his surprise, Jonathan's not there.

He's starting to get nervous, and feels a panic attack coming on, and just at the last moment when he's about to leave...Jonathan suddenly enters the studio. Steven is immediately relieved as he gives him a grateful hug and cheerfully says, "I'm really glad you made it." He hurriedly gets the studio ready to broadcast Jonathan's speech, and tells him about the upgraded software he uploaded that will allow him to override all current broadcasts. He shows Jonathan his mark, and he stands on it. Steven points at him and says, "Action!"

And with a very serious and sincere tone, he says, "My name is Jonathan Towers and I'm the leader of the NEL underground, and what I'm about to tell you is *extremely important!* I really need you to understand the urgency of this problem! And if parents truly care about your children, then you should really listen to what I have to say, "You must stop ignoring and realize the fact that carbon dioxide pollution, from burning fossil fuels, and deforestation are severely damaging the environment and affecting your health.

We need to join together and take a stand against the NWA, and end these deadly threats to our civilization...I know we were all taught to believe that the petroleum industry is making our life more convenient, and it has to some extent, but at a very costly price. We are all biologically connected, and a part of this complex eco system that sustains organic life on Earth. So we must stop damaging it!" He pauses for a brief moment and continues, "*You must* realize that it's extremely more important to keep our Air, Water, and Earth free from the harmful effects of carbon poisons and chemical pollutants, than it is to continuing using petroleum technology...*You must protect the environment*, animals, and insects that maintain the fragile natural balance of this Earth.

Anything that threatens our natural resources is the *true enemy*! *You must* learn to live in harmony with nature, and live together with each other as true equals, with mutually caring respect, like what Jesus spoke about...No more of this selfish, greedy, murderous mindset of people thinking they deserve more than another because their smarter or stronger. As long as you are contributing the same amount of effort utilizing what skills you may have, no matter how great or minimal they may be, then you shall equally receive all the necessary life sustaining natural resources. *Everybody* gets what they need!" He hesitates for a moment, and then with strong enthusiasm says, "I know it might sound difficult, but I know it can be done. We can concentrate our efforts to make the necessary changes, even though they may be extreme, and *Shut down this petroleum industrial monster*! I truly believe we can stop the damage to the Earth and show God we care about this planet."

He sadly stares into the camera and continues,
"So please take a moment and search deep
inside yourselves and try to hear the voice of
humanity that's silently screaming; Stop
abusing the Planet!"
And if you can't hear it, then listen harder,
because it's there!"
And then with an urgent tone as if he's pleading
to someone in the past says,
"If everyone can come together, like what
President Roosevelt did during WWII, and
retool all the automotive factories to only make
electric vehicles, and *eliminate all combustion
engines*! This will dramatically help stop the
damage to the Earth, and be a major step
towards turning this planet into the Utopian
Eden it was meant to be... That's how *you* can
possibly stop this destructive train that society
currently on...If you don't want to live in this
treacherous world, like the one we live in, than
make the necessary changes NOW!"

Brian was outside the studio watching, mesmerized, as he listened to Jonathan's speech. When suddenly the highly aggravated search party comes aggressively running down the hallway and commands him to "freeze." He quickly opens the studio door and frantically yells, "They're coming. Save yourselves!!" The guards mercilessly gun down poor confused Brian.

Acknowledgments...

I would like to acknowledge all the people throughout history, who have stood up for truth and righteousness. I want to thank my Aunt for her support with this project.
And most of all, I would like to thank Yeshua for his courage and sacrifice.

Made in the USA
San Bernardino, CA
16 February 2020